The Greatest Gift

S.L. STERLING

The Greatest Gift

Copyright © 2021 by S.L. Sterling

All rights reserved. Without limiting the rights under copyright reserved about, no part of this publication may be reproduced, stored in, or introduced into a retrieval system, or transmitted in any form or by any means (mechanical, electronic, photocopying, recording, or otherwise) without the prior written permission of both the copyright owner and the above publisher of the book. This is a work of fiction. Any references to historical events, real people, or real places are used fictitiously. Other names, characters, places, and events are products of the author's imagination, and any resemblance to actual events or places or persons, living or dead, is entirely coincidental. Disclaimer: This book contains mature content not suitable for those under the age of 18. It involves strong language and sexual situations. All parties portrayed in sexual situations are consenting adults over the age of 18.

ISBN: 978-1-989566-29-9

Paperback ISBN: 978-1-989566-30-5

Editor: Brandi Aquino, Editing Done Write

Cover Design: Thunderstruck Cover Design

The Greatest Gift

USA Today Bestselling Author
S.L. STERLING

Prologue

TESS

"What do you think? It's a little much isn't it?" I said, staring down at the gold accents that lined the entire table. I brought my finger up to my lips in thought and twisted my head to the left to see if it looked any better.

Laura let out a giggle. "A little much? You can twist your head any way you want, it will still look like a leprechaun threw up in here. I told you, subtle hints of gold."

Laura was not only my best friend and my maid of honor for my upcoming wedding; she was also one of the best interior designers in the area, so when she offered to help me get things ready for our Thanksgiving celebration, I jumped at it. "Geez, thanks. I just want everything to be perfect for the family this holiday."

Derrick and I had been engaged for two years, and we

had finally settled on a date. Since some of the relatives would not be able to make it to the wedding, I had decided to hold a pre-wedding Thanksgiving party. It would be a chance for everyone to get together prior to the wedding, since right after we were married, we were headed to Paris for our honeymoon over Christmas and New Years.

"I understand, but seriously, you have got to tone it down, get rid of some things because..." Laura stuck her finger down her throat in a mock gag, and then smiled at me.

I looked at the table again, agreeing with her. "Okay, I agree. It's a little much." We both laughed. She quickly grabbed a box and went about removing everything that needed to go, rearranging other things as she went.

"Do you have everything finalized for the wedding now? I can always help you out with that as well. I know it's coming down to crunch time."

"Yep, everything has been booked and finalized. I just confirmed numbers with the caterer this morning. Oh, and I put the last payment down on the honeymoon this morning. We cannot wait to spend ten days in Paris. Now, just cross your fingers that nothing happens that forces us to have to cancel that trip."

Laura raised a brow. "Well, unless Derrick decides to throw another one of his stellar fits, I doubt you need to worry about cancelling."

Derrick hadn't really wanted to go to Paris; he'd wanted to spend our honeymoon in Vale, skiing, but I had worked out a compromise with him and had decided that partway through our Paris vacation we would uproot and go to one of the ski resorts there. He'd listened to my idea, and after voicing his displeasure in front of the entire wedding party, he had reluctantly agreed to the trip.

"Oh, I wouldn't say I don't have to worry about it," I said, looking down at the table, adjusting a few more things. "I sort of negotiated a deal, but in order to take it, I had to waive our rights to a refund," I said, biting my lower lip and looking at my best friend, who shoved the box of gold accents at me to repackage.

Her eyes bugged. "Tess! Derrick is going to flip out. That's a lot of money to spend on a trip with no chance of getting your money back."

"I know," I cried, "but it was such a good deal, and with all the money we are already spending, it just kind of made sense. Besides, I am the one paying for the honeymoon. It's coming from my savings. He agreed to pay for the wedding if I took care of the honeymoon."

Laura tilted her head and gave me a knowing look, making me feel unsure about my decision. "I know, Tess, but seriously, I'd hate for something to happen and you to lose out. Derrick won't be happy. You know how he gets."

"I know, you're right, but just do me one little favor and don't mention anything to Derrick about it."

"Tess, I wouldn't do that. What stays between you and I does exactly that. However, on that note, you better make it up to me by bring me lots of pictures, because your trip looks like it will be amazing. I checked everything out the other night after you sent me all the info."

"It does look amazing, doesn't it?" I giggled, excitement filling me. "Staying in that old hotel, it will be the oldest building I've stayed in. I just wish that Derrick would change his mind about dinner in the Eiffel Tower."

"Just keep working on him. Perhaps he will bend. You don't happen to have the gift bags for the guest gifts, do you? I have to put these in." She held up the thank you cards.

"Oh yes, now where did I put them?" I questioned under my breath, looking around the dining room, and that was when I spotted the box. "They are right over there against the wall." I stood pointing to the box that sat beside the fireplace.

Laura wandered over and opened the box and let out a small giggle as she held up one of the gift bags. "Gold bags? Really, Tess?"

"Oh God, I totally forgot I ordered them," I said, burying my face in my hands. "All right, we definitely need to tone down the gold." I laughed.

Laura had just finished packing up the last of the Thanksgiving gift bags, while I repackaged all the gold accents, when the front door slammed shut and Derrick walked in. He stood in the doorway to the dining room in his suit and trench coat, holding his laptop bag. "What's going on in here?" he questioned, looking at us both.

"Just getting things ready for Thanksgiving." I smiled, holding up one gift bag, letting it swing back and forth in between my fingers.

"Gift bags? What are those for?" Derrick questioned.

"The guests, silly," I said, going over to kiss him hello, only instead of kissing me back, he turned his head and my lips landed on his cheek.

"Gift bags for Thanksgiving dinner? Little much, don't you think?" I could hear the annoyance in his voice.

I nodded my head. "Yes, of course, but it's only because most of them can't be at the wedding."

"Tess, it was their choice not to be at the wedding. We don't need to hand out gift bags at a family dinner."

I glanced over to Laura, who stood there pretending to sort through one of the boxes. I could tell she was uncomfortable. "Fine, Derrick, I will rethink the bags."

Laura glanced up at us. "Okay, guys, I guess that is my cue. I'm out of here. I'll be back tomorrow to help you finish up with this," she said, slipping her shoes on and grabbing her purse. I had planned to invite her for dinner, but, given Derrick's attitude, I knew she wouldn't stay so I decided against it. I walked her to the door and waved as she climbed into her car and backed out of the driveway.

I closed and locked the front door and walked over to

where Derrick stood still looking in at the stuff in the dining room. "What did you want to do tonight? I figured we could just stay in, curl up in front of the fire, and watch a movie, but if you have something else in mind, I'm all ears," I said, reaching up and pulling at the knot of his tie to loosen it.

He grabbed my hands, removing them from his body, and cleared his throat. "I have some work to finish up first. I'll be awhile," he barked, and without another word, he climbed the stairs to his office. "Oh and get rid of those gift bags, they aren't needed."

"Okay, well, I'll get dinner going," I called up, but instead of a response, I heard nothing but the slam of his office door. I shrugged, wondering what was bothering him but figured that he'd had a bad day and needed to decompress, so without another word, I left him alone and made my way into the kitchen to start dinner.

A little after seven, I yelled up to Derrick letting him know dinner was ready. When I didn't get a response, I climbed a couple of steps then heard him on the phone. I assumed he was speaking with a client, so I made my way back down to the kitchen. I had our dinner already plated and had already started eating when he walked into the kitchen ten minutes later. He still wore his black dress pants and white dress shirt; the only thing missing was his tie. He sat down in his usual spot, picked up his fork, and dug into the salad without saying a word.

"How was your day?" I asked.

"Fine." He grumbled.

"That's it, fine?"

"Yes, Tess, that is it. Finance can be a boring business. Tell me, what are you doing with all that stuff in the dining room? There must be over five hundred dollars worth of useless garbage in there."

"I told you, it's for Thanksgiving. It didn't cost that much. Laura let me use her discount, and most of it is returnable. I just figured we could make this meal a little special, that's all. Besides, it's more for the people who couldn't make the wedding more than anything."

"I told you, it was their decision not to come. What was in the gift bags?" he questioned.

"Gifts, of course. Just a little thank you for coming to dinner," I said, smiling, only I noticed immediately that Derrick didn't smile back. "Is something wrong?"

Derrick let out a huff, "Never mind. It's nothing," he mumbled, picking up his wineglass and drinking down the contents.

"Oh, I have good news."

"What's that?"

I paid for the honeymoon today. I also called the hotel and asked them to upgrade our room to the honeymoon package. Oh, and I got notification for the flight. No times yet, but it's confirmed."

Derrick avoided eye contact with me while I continued. "Oh, and the train over to Le Mont-Dore has been booked as well. I know you had mentioned wanting to ski more, but the resort didn't have any openings until the twenty-ninth, and that day we will spend most of it on a train. I did my best." When I looked back up and at Derrick, I noticed he wasn't paying attention to a word I'd said. Instead he sat there with a far-off look in his eyes. I frowned. "Derrick, what is it?"

"What?"

"Come on, you've barely looked at me, and have barely said two words since you came down here. I was telling you about the trip and skiing, and you said nothing. What is going on? Is something wrong at work?"

Derrick blew out a breath and looked up at the ceiling. Something was on his mind, and I watched as he struggled with whatever it was. It was like he didn't want to tell me.

"Tess, I have something to tell you, and to be honest, I do not know how I am going to say it."

I blew out a breath, my stomach in knots. "Derrick, we talked a long time ago about this. Bad news is just best to be said. Then we deal with whatever it is together. So, what is it?" I gave him my undivided attention, thinking perhaps he had lost an enormous deal at work and wanted someone to talk to.

He sat there, his eyes locked with mine, a line etched between his brows. "There is no easy way to say this, Tess," he said hanging his head. "I, um, I met someone, and she is everything I've ever wanted."

"You what?" Instantly, I felt my body heat, and the room got dark, my surroundings spinning, making me feel lightheaded.

"I meant someone. I don't want to get married."

I had no idea what to say as I sat there staring down at my plate, the contents of my stomach threatening to come back up. I swallowed hard, picked up my wineglass, and was about to take a sip, but the smell of the wine made my stomach turn faster than it already was. I put my glass down and took a deep breath, he had to be joking. There was no way he was serious.

A small smile came to my lips. "You're joking, right? Who put you up to this, Laura? One of the boys? It was Maddox, wasn't it? He's the one who's always playing practical jokes. Or wait, maybe it was Pace," I said, laughing, because otherwise the tears were going to start falling. Only Derrick didn't laugh. He sat there looking at me without an ounce of emotion on his face.

"I'm serious, Tess. It's not a joke. I don't think it's fair that I lead you on, so I'm doing what is best for both of us. We are going to cancel the wedding. It will save us both a messy divorce later on down the road."

My eyes burned as I looked at him. There wasn't a hint of a smile on his face; he was serious. He didn't want to get married. I looked down at the ring that sat on my finger, the large diamond that I had always said was too big for me staring back at me. I couldn't find words to say to him. Hurt, rage and anger filled me. I sat there staring at him, even though the sight of him was making me sick.

"We've paid for everything," I murmured.

"We have a cancellation policy on almost all of it. I'll call the venue and caterers in the morning. I'll more than likely lose the security deposit, but that isn't a big deal considering the alternative." He shrugged, getting up from the table, throwing his napkin down on top of his half-eaten dinner. "You should call and cancel the trip. We won't be needing it anymore. Since the house is yours, I will pack up my things and be out by the end of the week." He shoved his chair under the table and left the kitchen. I could hear him make his way upstairs.

With tears in my eyes, I grabbed the dishes from the table. When I heard his office door slam shut, I smashed the dishes into the sink and closed my eyes tightly. I breathed deeply and opened my eyes, standing there looking down at the mess of broken dishes and half-eaten food lying in the sink as tears poured down my cheeks.

I woke late the following morning and lay in bed listening to the silence of the house. I'd heard Derrick leave the house around six this morning, more than likely to head to the office, or perhaps to go to her, whomever she was. He hadn't come to bed last night, and for that I'd been grateful. There would have been no way I could have slept beside him.

I lay under the heavy blankets staring at the wall of our bedroom, his side of the bed cold, when I heard the doorbell ring. I didn't have an ounce of energy, and I really didn't want to see anyone, so I just stayed in bed, pretending I wasn't home. Then I remembered that I'd parked my car in the driveway and not the garage. Whoever was at the door would know I was home. I let out a sigh and heard the doorbell ring again for a second time.

I didn't bother to get dressed. I just kicked the covers off myself and made my way down the stairs. I pulled the door open to see Laura standing there, a smile on her face, until she laid eyes on me. Her eyes ran down my pajama-clad body. "Are you sick?" she questioned, frowning as she reached out and smoothed down my hair, which I was sure was a disaster.

I didn't answer her, just shrugged.

"What is the matter with you? Did you forget we were going to take some of that stuff back today and get some different accent pieces for the dinner table?"

"Doesn't matter anymore," I muttered and turned to make my way into the kitchen, leaving Laura standing in the front door.

I put the kettle on and dumped the old coffee grounds out of my French press into the garbage. I added three tablespoons of grounds and turned to see Laura standing in the kitchen's doorway watching me.

"What is going on? You are acting really strange. Did someone die? Should I call Derrick? Perhaps he should come home." She reached for her phone and started searching her contacts.

"The wedding is off," I murmured, turning, my eyes full of tears.

Laura's eyes bulged out of her head as she heard the words leave my lips. "What? Oh my God, Tess." She immediately walked over to me and wrapped her arms around me.

"We have to cancel everything," I muttered as tears poured down my cheeks. "I have to call the caterer and the venue, and oh God, I have to call all the guests." I cried into her shoulder.

"What happened?"

I swallowed hard as the kettle whistled. "He found someone else and figures it's better to not get married."

"That good for nothing, lying asshole!" Laura yelled, stomping her foot. "Did he say who?"

I shook my head while she wrapped her arms around me, squeezing me tight, doing her best to comfort me. It didn't matter who he had met. I didn't care to know. All I wanted was for him to get out of the house and be gone out of my life.

Laura and I sat in the living room working on calling all the guests. Derrick carried the last few boxes of his stuff down the stairs, followed by Maddox, who'd agreed to help him move. Derrick marched out the door without another word, we had done nothing but argue since he had arrived. Maddox placed the box he'd been carrying on the floor and then poked his head into the living room.

"I think that is it, Tess. Just call me if he forgot anything and I'll come by and pick it up."

I looked up at him and nodded. "Okay, thanks, but please don't let him come with you. I don't want to see him again," I said, standing up and going over to him.

"I won't bring him back here. I promise. You can call me if you need anything." He smiled, pulling me in for a hug.

Maddox and Derrick had been best friends growing up. The couple of years I had been with Derrick, Maddox had become a very good friend to me. He was someone I cherished, and I hoped that with the news of us breaking up meant that he, too, wouldn't disappear from my life.

"Let's go," I heard Derrick call from outside.

"He beckons." He gave me a half smile and rolled his eyes. "Guess I've got to go," Maddox said, winking at me. He leaned in and placed a gentle kiss on my cheek. "I'm on holidays for the next week, so if you're feeling lonely, just call or text, okay."

I nodded and watched as he walked out the front door, pulling it shut behind him.

I went in and flopped down on the couch just as Laura crossed off another name on the list and hung up her phone. "Another person off the list," she said, smiling.

I pinched the bridge of my nose. "I guess I should now call and try to cancel that trip. Even if I won't get my money back, perhaps they can offer me some sort of credit."

Laura looked up from the list of names and shook her head. "No way. Don't you dare."

"Don't cancel the trip?" I questioned, rubbing the tension from my neck.

"That's right. I was speaking with your mom earlier. Her and I both agree that you should go on that trip, regardless. It will give you a chance to get over everything that has gone on, perhaps even give you a new outlook on things. Call it a self-discovery trip."

I looked at her. She was being ridiculous. "Yeah, okay, let me get this straight. I'm to go on my honeymoon by myself to get over my fiancé dumping me eight weeks before our wedding? That doesn't exactly shout fun," I said, rolling my eyes. I picked up the confirmation email I had printed and searched it to find the number I needed to call and cancel.

I'd just found it when the front door opened, and I heard my mother call out a hello. I looked at Laura and gritted my teeth, not really in the mood to be ambushed by either of them. "Hey, Mom. We're in here," I called out.

Mom came around the corner, a huge smile on her face. "Okay, girls, tell me what I can do to help?" she asked, throwing her coat and purse over the arm of the couch.

"You can convince your daughter to go on that trip, while I continue to call and let guests know they cancelled the wedding," Laura said, looking proud of herself.

Mom looked at me with disappointment written all over her face. Then she sat down and crossed her arms. I could tell from her body language that I was about to get a lecture. "Tess, you paid for that trip. You should at least go. I know how excited you were to go see Paris. Besides, it will do you good to get out of here for a while and away from all of this."

I shrugged and looked at Laura. "You two don't get it. I don't want to go. This should have been my honeymoon. How much fun do you think I am going to have? First, I'll be alone, and second, it's only going to be a reminder of what would have been."

Mom and Laura looked at one another, suddenly smiling as if they had an idea.

"What?" I asked, crossing my arms and rolling my eyes.

"So don't go alone. Take one of your friends. What about Laura?" Mom asked.

"Oh, no, I can't go. I'm heading out to Denver for Christmas. Going to visit my parents," Laura said, putting the phone down on the table.

"Okay, so we need to find someone to go with you. Your father and I cannot go. We have plans already—Hawaii." Mom brought her finger up to her lips and squinted her eyes as she tried to think of someone. Suddenly, her eyes lit up. "What about one of your single, platonic male friends?"

I put my head in my hands and shook it before running my fingers through my hair. "Mom, I don't have single male friends."

"There has to be someone, Tess."

"Like who?" I frowned.

"Teddy, or perhaps the firefighter, oh what's his name? You know the one with those stunning blue eyes?" Mom said, once again bringing her finger to her lips as she struggled to come up with his name.

"Maddox?" I questioned.

"Yes, that's it, Maddox! He has always adored you. You should ask him," Mom said, Laura nodding in agreement.

"You actually just missed him." Laura smiled.

"Oh, that is too bad. I've always liked him, such a sweet man, and a good looking one too."

I buried my face in my hands. I couldn't believe that, as I stood here, my mother and Laura were plotting to fix me up with someone so I could go on this trip. I rolled my eyes. "Mom, Maddox isn't even my friend. He is Derrick's."

"Now I know for a fact that isn't true. Maddox adores spending time with you," Laura interjected. "Did you see the way he hugged you earlier? And he is single."

I gritted my teeth and looked toward Laura, willing her with my eyes to stop. "Don't you have a list of people in front of you to call?" I interjected.

"Right, phone calls." She giggled as she picked up the phone and began dialling.

Mom turned to me. "Oh, Tess, don't be so stubborn. I agree. I think you need to go on that trip, but I don't want my daughter travelling halfway across the country alone. Plus, everyone else has plans, and if Maddox is single…and willing to go…then I don't see any reason why you shouldn't ask him."

I picked up the other half of the guest list and shoved it at my mother without answering her. "I'll go make us some coffee. I am sure it is going to be a late night," I said, leaving the room and heading out to kitchen.

"Just ask him?" she yelled out as I left the room.

"Mother, please, I am not asking Maddox!" I shouted over my shoulder.

"I'm just saying..." She smiled and lifted her eyebrows in gest. "He's a good-looking guy who would probably love to accompany you to Paris. Just ask him."

I shook my head in disbelief that my own mother would even suggest such a thing. I could hear them giggle from the kitchen, and I shook my head as their suggestion ran through my mind. "Ridiculously crazy," I muttered to myself as I made the coffee for everyone. There was no way I was asking anyone to go on that trip with me, if I were to go at all.

Maddox

The solid red of brake lights in front of me added to my frustration level as I swerved in and out of lanes. I'd been over at Tess's helping her move a piece of furniture when I'd remembered I'd had dinner plans with Derrick in the city, and now I sat in gridlock. I was extremely late.

He had called me earlier through the week, wanting to know if I would be available tonight. He'd been distant and non-social since his split with Tess. I had tried to talk some sense into him the night I helped him move, and I figured that perhaps some of things I had said had sunk in and he had come to his senses. I figured he wanted to get together to work through a plan on ways to repair their relationship and get her back. My cell phone rang just as the traffic light turned red, and I slammed on my brakes to avoid going through it.

"Hey, man, where are you?" Derrick questioned.

"Don't ask. I'm stuck in traffic. It's getting worse every night that passes. I swear the holiday shoppers are already out. This city is literally in gridlock," I uttered as the guy in front of me slammed on his brakes to avoid ramming into the car in front of him. "Fuck you!" I yelled as I swerved just in time to avoid colliding into the backside of his car. "Just order without me. I'll get there when I get there." I groaned, completely frustrated.

"No way. We don't want to do that."

"We?" I asked, making sure I heard him correctly. When Derrick had called, he hadn't mentioned that anyone else would be joining us.

"Yes, I have someone I want you to meet."

I rolled my eyes; guess I was wrong about what Derrick had wanted. Honestly, I was disgusted with my best friend. He'd been engaged to Tess for two years, and a year ago, he started acting strange. There had been times they were to meet for dinner, and at the last second, he would call me in a panic and ask me to go meet her because he couldn't get there on time. Other times, he'd asked me to cover for him so he could go away on the weekend. The first couple of times I did as he asked, figuring that he was planning a surprise for Tess, but I'd been wrong. Instead, I was unknowingly covering for him every time he wanted to screw around on her.

I'd never forget the night I found out, either. I'd

received a call a little after eleven from an extremely panicked Tess, who had been trying for hours to get hold of him. So, I'd done what any decent friend would do and got in my truck and drove to his office.

I'd taken the elevator up to the twentieth floor and made my way down the halls to his office. I could see the soft glow of light through the blinds of his enclosed office, and without any thought, I'd pushed the door open. Only he wasn't alone. His secretary had her legs wrapped around his neck while his face was buried between them. I could remember the shock on his face as he saw me. We'd had words, and I basically told him to tell Tess or I would.

He'd begged me not to tell her and hung his head in shame, explaining he was going through a rough patch, and this was the one and only time he would do this. He was my best friend, and I trusted him and hoped that after I'd caught him, it would bring him back to reality. I'd heard nothing of it again, until I got a call from him three weeks ago asking me to help him move out.

"I'll be there as soon as I can be."

The second Derrick hung up, I threw my phone down into the console and sat back, staring straight ahead at the traffic. I tapped my thumb on the wheel. I had no desire to meet Lucy. I really had no desire to even sit down and eat dinner with him now, but I was committed, and unlike him, I didn't go back on my word.

I was about to pull into the other lane when my phone

vibrated against the dash. Laura's name flashed on my screen. I frowned as I picked up the phone, reading her text.

You busy for Christmas?

I frowned and went to text her back when the traffic began to move, so instead I called her.

"Why do you want to know what I'm doing for Christmas?" I asked the second she picked up her phone.

Laura let out a laugh. "Because Tess is heading to Paris, and she has no one to go with. I have plans with my family. Derrick has plans to screw whomever his dick is buried into this week, and her parents are on their way to Hawaii. I just figured that perhaps you might be free."

"I don't know, Laura. This kind of shit gets guys killed," I answered, chuckling into the phone.

"What? Why?"

"Um, do you not know about the infamous bro code?"

"Oh, please, don't feed me that line. You're her friend. Besides, does Derrick not know about the don't-screw-around-on-your-future-wife code?" she said in a mocking voice.

I chuckled. "Can I think about it?"

"Sure! I just thought I'd give you the heads up and let you know Tess may call and ask you to go."

"I was just at Tess's place. She mentioned nothing to me," I said, frowning.

"That's because she hasn't gotten the nerve yet, but trust me, I'm working on her." She giggled into the phone.

"All right, thanks for the heads up. I've got to go," I said, pulling into a parking spot outside of the restaurant.

"Okay, talk to you soon."

I pocketed my phone and paid for parking, then made my way inside, instantly spotting Derrick with a woman who couldn't even hold a candle to Tess.

"It's about time you got here," Derrick said, standing as I approached the table, holding his hand out for me to shake.

"Hey, man, sorry about that. Traffic was brutal," I said, removing my jacket and hanging it on the back of my chair while glancing to the woman who sat beside Derrick.

"No problem. Glad you could make it. Lucy, I'd like you to meet Maddox, my best friend." He grinned as he turned and placed his hand behind her as she stood up to shake my hand. "Maddox, this is Lucy."

After all the introductions, we ordered a few appetizers and drinks. I sat there listening to the two of them talking about some trip they were taking over Christmas. He'd apparently booked a ten-day getaway down to the Virgin Islands. Anger boiled in me as I sat there thinking about Tess and how she must be feeling, wondering if she even knew.

"How long have you known Derrick?" Lucy asked.

"Long enough," I muttered, looking to Derrick as he

held onto Lucy like he used to hold onto Tess. "We went to school together and then to college."

"Oh, so you've known one another for quite a long time. What was he like in school?"

I chuckled to myself. "He used to be quite the player in school," I bit out, glancing to Derrick, who sat there looking at me with shock on his face.

"Oh, is that so." Lucy smiled, looking over to Derrick like he was everything, thinking I was joking. However, Derrick just sat there and glared at me, his eyes turning dark.

"Yep, always had a woman on the go. Sometimes two or three at a time," I answered. "I could never keep up with who he was dating one week to the next."

"He's kidding, babe. He's quite the joker. Which reminds me, Maddox, could I see you for a moment? I wanted to run something by you," Derrick interjected, his jaw square and tight.

I grinned at him. "Is there a problem?" I asked, knowing very well he was pissed off and was using that as an excuse to pull me away from telling Lucy anything more.

"Now, Maddox," he spit, getting up from the table.

I downed my scotch, ice jingling against the glass as I set it down on the table with force. I stood up. "Lucy, please excuse us for a moment."

"Yes, please excuse us, darling." Derrick leaned down

to kiss her. "Why don't you order us all another drink, would you, darling? I just need to run something business related by Maddox here."

"Sure thing, babe," she said, looking up at him as he placed his hand under her chin, tilting her head back as he met her lips for a quick kiss.

I followed Derrick down the hall to the men's room and stopped just outside the door, turning to face him.

"What the fuck is your problem?" Derrick gritted.

"You seriously have to ask that? What the hell are you even doing? Jesus, you are supposed to be getting married in three weeks and heading to Paris, but instead you're planning some trip to some island with this piece."

"Look, I broke it off with Tess just like you wanted me to. Lucy is something special, but how would you ever understand?"

"What the fuck is that supposed to mean?"

"It means that since you are still single, you have no clue how it feels to be in love."

"Fuck you!" I said through clenched teeth, pushing my hands against his chest. Derrick knew what I had been through. How dare he even suggest something like that to me. "I don't think you know what it means to be in love. You had the perfect girl—the perfect fucking girl. Tess adored you, she would do anything for you, and stood by you during some of your worst fucking times, and you broke her heart like it meant nothing because you let your dick do the talking, just like you've always done. How long have you been doing this one?"

"Don't you dare talk to me like that!"

"Why the hell not? Because the truth hurts? Honestly, I do not know what the hell you are even doing with this chick or even where you found her. She doesn't even begin to hold a candle to Tess. She is just another fucking bimbo, just like all the rest of them."

"Well, you better get used to the fucking bimbo, because I'm asking her to marry me tonight."

"You're what?" I blurted, my eyes almost falling out of my head. The bed he and Tess slept in hadn't even grown cold, and here he was talking about marrying some other chick.

"You heard me. I have the ring in my pocket. I wanted you to be here for it."

I scratched my head, barely believing what I was hearing. "Well, Derrick, I hate to break it to you, but I don't want to be here for it. I won't stand beside you either at this wedding or any other for that fact, so don't even fucking ask me. The best thing I could do for that girl right now is walk out there and warn her about you."

We stood there staring at one another for what felt like an eternity, then without another word, Derrick turned and made his way back to the table. I took a minute to cool off before making my way back to the table to find Derrick holding Lucy's hand and speaking in a low voice to her, as both of them smiled at one another. I pulled my phone from my pocket and placed it on the table, staring down at the screen to avoid being sick at the disgusting display in front of me. I was just about to tell them I was going to head out when my phone vibrated against the table, Tess's name flashing on the screen.

"Would you two please excuse me for a moment? I have to take this call." I grabbed my phone before Derrick could see who it was and made my way to the front door of the restaurant. I pushed the door open and walked out into the frosty night air.

"Hey, Tess. What's up."

"Hey, Maddox. I'm not bothering you, am I? I mean, I know you had dinner plans, so if it's a bad time, I can always call back later."

"Not at all. What's up?" I inquired, glancing over my shoulder to make sure Derrick hadn't followed me outside.

"Well, I know you just left, but I was wondering if you could pop by tonight after you finish your dinner? I have something I wanted to run by you."

I pinched the bridge of my nose and turned to glance back into the window of the restaurant at where Derrick and Lucy sat. I blinked hard as I watched Derrick pull a small black box from his jacket pocket, while Lucy brought her hands up to cover her mouth. I rolled my eyes; that poor girl had no idea that he broke off his last engagement only a few weeks before. I felt bad for her, but I felt really bad for Tess. She'd be crushed knowing he had already moved on without any regard. I knew I should have called her the night I found him the first time, but she was such a beautiful woman. I didn't want to be the one to break her heart. Instead, I had hoped that my friend had been telling me the truth and would have come clean himself.

"Maddox, are you there? I didn't lose you, did I? Are you in a bad cell area?"

"Sorry, no, I'm here. I have zero plans after dinner tonight, and I can't think of a better way to spend an evening," I said as I watched Lucy wrap her arms around Derrick's neck and then look at the ring that she had slipped onto her finger. "Give me an hour. I'll be on my way."

Tess

It was almost eight and my nerves filled my stomach as I looked at the clock. I was sure Maddox would be here any minute, so I shoved the last of my dinner in my mouth and cleared my plate from the table. I put the dishes in the dishwasher, then quickly washed the pot in the sink before leaving it to dry. I grabbed my sweater from the back of my chair, shut the kitchen light off, and made my way into the living room where I lit a candle and turned on the TV.

I sat down on the couch and rung my hands together. I didn't know why I was even bothering to give in to Laura's crazy idea of asking Maddox to go with me. I knew it was more to keep Laura and my mom off my back. Neither of them thought I should travel to Paris alone, even though I insisted I would be fine.

Maddox had become more of a friend to me than I

had originally thought. Since Derrick and I had separated, he had spent nights with me when the girls weren't able to. When I asked him why, he said he was doing what he could to make sure I wasn't spending a lot of time alone. He had been the only one of Derrick's friends who had been coming around regularly to help me and spend time with me, and for that, I was grateful. Some of the others had only come around to take advantage of my broken heart.

When I saw the lights of his truck shine through the front windows, I ran back into the kitchen and switched the coffee on. I had just pulled mugs from the cupboard when I heard a knock at the door. "Come on in..." I called.

"Hey, Tess, it's just me," his deep voice echoed down the hall.

"Oh, hey," I stammered, peaking my head around the corner in time to see Maddox take his coat off and hang it up on the coat rack. "Did you want anything to snack on? I was just going to put some chips in a bowl, and I'm making coffee."

"Sounds great," he said, stepping into the kitchen. "Sorry I am late. Traffic was bad coming in from the city," he whispered, wrapping his arms around me in one of his brotherly hugs. Over the past few weeks, I'd come to love those hugs.

"No big deal. It shocked me when you said you were free tonight. Normally, you'd be out with Derrick. I figured that was where you were off to when you said you had to meet someone for dinner."

"No, not tonight. I met up with an old friend for a quick bite, and then I had a couple errands to run," he said, letting me go, his jaw tense.

"His loss is my gain I guess." I giggled, emptying the bag of chips into the bowl and pouring two cups of coffee. I was about to pick up the two mugs and carry them to the table when Maddox stepped beside me.

"Let me," he said, reaching in front of me, picking up the mugs in his large, muscular hands. He carried them over to the table while I followed with the bowl of chips.

"What did you want to do tonight? A movie?" he asked.

"Um, sure, but first I wanted to talk to you about something."

"Yes, you said something about that. Okay, shoot." Maddox grinned, pulling out a chair at the table, straddling it.

"Well, I feel sort of silly asking you, and please don't feel obligated to say yes."

"Okay." He chuckled.

"Really, I mean it. If you are busy, or think it's stupid, just say so and we will move on and forget I even asked," I said, toying with a lock of my hair.

"Tess."

"Seriously, I hate to do this…" I said, uncertainty filling

my voice while sitting down across from him, taking a sip of my coffee.

"Tess," he repeated.

I met his eyes and then lowered mine to the floor. "I mean it, Maddox."

"How about you ask me whatever it is you want to ask, and we will take it from there?" He chuckled, shoving a couple of chips into his mouth.

"Well, um, I had to keep the trip to Paris. I made a stupid mistake and booked the trip on a discount and had to give up the refund option. So I had to keep it. Besides, I paid for the damn thing and was so excited about going," I said, trying to justify to myself why I should go. "Anyway, my mom and Laura were making a big deal of me going alone. They don't think it's a good idea for me to travel alone, so I thought perhaps I'd ask and see if you'd like to go with me."

"Just let me check my work schedule. I think I'm only working one or two of the days you are going. I know there are guys that will kill for the hours, especially at this time of year, so..." he said, pulling his phone out and searching through his contacts.

"Oh, forget it, this is just stupid. My mother and Laura both think I need someone to go with, but I'll be fine. I'll be totally fine. You don't have to go. You probably already have plans with your family or something. I have no idea what I'm even doing. Seriously, Maddox, just forget that I asked," I stammered and got up from my chair and began pacing back and forth while I fiddled with my earring.

"Whoa, Tess, calm down. I'd love to go."

"Really?" I faltered, meeting his eyes.

"Yes, really." He smiled, standing, coming over to me and placing his hands on my shoulders. "I just need to make a couple of calls."

As Maddox walked away, I wondered if perhaps I was putting him into an uncomfortable position, what with being Derrick's best friend, and I worried that he might feel the same.

"Maddox?"

He glanced over his shoulder at me. "Yeah."

"I'm not putting you in an uncomfortable position, am I? I mean, your friendship with Derrick. He's going to be upset, I am sure of that."

Maddox shrugged. "Let me worry about that, okay. I'm just going to make a couple of calls and see if I can get those two shifts covered. Give me...oh, I don't know, about ten minutes." He nodded and checked his watch.

"Okay." I looked away as he got up and made his way into the dining room. I stood inside the kitchen watching him. His back was turned to me and he ran his hand through his hair as he dialled a number. He was mid-conversation when he turned around and saw me watching him. I smiled, then grabbed the bowl of chips and our coffees and carried them into the living room and curled up on the couch, flipping through the channels while waiting for him to return. When he did, a smile lined his lips.

"All right, we are all set." He grinned, sitting down on the couch beside me. "We are going to Paris."

I smiled. "YAY! Oh, wait, we should get your name on the tickets." I was excited that I would not have to spend what would have been my honeymoon alone. I knew deep down that if I went alone, I would spend my time moping around the hotel room feeling sorry for myself.

"Sounds good. Why don't we take care of that now and then figure out what we are going to do while we are there. We can search some sites, look for restaurants, museums, and things that you'd like to see and really lay out a plan."

"That would be great." I grinned and reached for my laptop, setting it on the table in front of me.

All it took was a single phone call to the travel agent, and everything had been switched from Derrick's name and into Maddox's name. It was a simple procedure, and then the travel agent sent over a few links to some local events for us to check out.

While I sat there going over the websites that the travel agent had sent, Maddox tapped me on the shoulder. "What is it?" I questioned.

"Did you notice that we are flying out of a different

airport?" A look of confusion lining his face as he shuffled the travel documents around.

I huffed, annoyed at the entire reason. "Well, you will love this. Derrick wanted to ski, so we are spending some of the trip in a private chalet near some huge ski resort. We take a train from Paris to Le-Mont Dore on the seventh day of the trip, and we spend New Year's Eve there."

He frowned. "Well, Tess, that sounds fabulous, but I'm a little confused."

I could tell from the look on his face what was coming, yet I pretended not to. "What are you confused about?" I asked innocently.

"Tess, even I know you don't ski. So, I'm confused why you wouldn't be spending your entire trip in Paris?"

I squirmed in my seat and looked down at my mug. "Do you want a top up?" I asked, standing up.

"Sure, but first, I'd like you to answer my question? Why wouldn't you be spending your entire trip in Paris?" he questioned, pulling at my arm, making me sit back down.

I looked at him, then lowered my eyes and shook my head. "It was the only way he would agree to go to Paris."

Maddox sat silently for a moment, thinking over what I'd said. "Let me guess, he wanted to go to Vail or something like that."

I nodded. "If I hadn't of come up with some sort of compromise, he would have spent everyday all day on the slopes, and I would have been left to my own devices." I shrugged. "As it was, he was irritated that we'd only be there for a couple of days."

Maddox shook his head. I could tell he didn't know how to respond to what I had just told him. I hadn't even told Laura about this. She thought we would be spending the entire time in the heart of Paris.

"Don't worry about it, Maddox. Why don't you look at the skiing while I go refill our mugs." My lips trembling, I got up, took our mugs, and made my way into the kitchen so that I didn't break down in tears.

When I returned to the living room, Maddox sat on the couch surfing on his phone. "Okay, so I was just looking. They have ski lessons, so why don't we sign you up for some lessons while we are there? That way you're not spending your time alone."

I shook my head. "No, I think I will just book another spa day for myself." I shrugged.

"Come on, I'd even do them with you, if it will make you feel better."

"Ha, have you seen me on feet?" I laughed. "Things that slide aren't my friend."

"Come on, if you don't feel comfortable with that, I could give you lessons if you prefer. You could think of me as your own private ski instructor," he said, knocking my shoulder. "It's really easy."

"For someone with balance, yes, it's easy." I giggled. "I

just prefer that you enjoy yourself. Please don't worry about me. Like I said, I'll just book in for another spa day or go shopping while you're gone. You don't need to be with me every single second."

"You're sure?"

"I am positive. I want you to enjoy your trip as well."

Maddox studied me for a moment and then turned his eyes onto the computer and began changing the name on Derrick's ski pass to his.

Maddox

It was Friday night, and Tess and I walked through the mall together, wandering in and out of shops, looking for things for the trip. I'd needed a few things for skiing, and Tess had been more than happy to go with me so she could get some stuff for the trip as well. She'd just come out of the drugstore carrying a bag and walked over to me. "Okay, I think I got everything I needed from there." She smiled, while checking things off her list.

"Did you get the condoms?" I questioned with a serious look on my face.

Her eyes bulged out of her head, and her cheeks went red as she looked at me. I couldn't help but burst into laughter at the look on her face. "I'm just kidding, sweetie." I chuckled, grabbing her and pulling her into my side as she laughed. "Well, not really, but..."

"You are sick." She giggled.

"Yeah, but I made you laugh didn't I?"

She bit her bottom lip and nodded. "You did."

I glanced over her head at one store, an idea coming to mind. "Would you like to get a hot chocolate before we continue on?" I questioned, nodding to the only chocolate shop in the mall.

"That sounds good, actually, but not from there. Let's just go to the coffee shop. It's right around the corner." She pointed, but I took off into the chocolate shop, while she stood in the mall.

I wanted to treat her and thank her somehow for the trip because I knew there was no way she was going to let me pay for my ticket. I could hear her behind me trying to stop me, but I ignored her pleas and placed the order anyway, and by the time she reached the counter, the girl was already busy making our drinks.

"I don't need a ten-dollar hot chocolate, Maddox," she said, placing her hand on my arm.

"Have you ever had one of these?" I asked, ignoring what she said. "They are freaking delicious."

She shook her head. "Derrick thought they were a waste of money." She shrugged. "So, no, I've never tried one. Here..." she said, fishing through her purse and pulling out a ten-dollar bill and handing it to me.

"What is that for?" I frowned, looking to the bill in her hand and back to her eyes.

"The hot chocolate." She shrugged.

"Not going to happen. I wanted to get it for you, and all I ask is that you enjoy it. So, you are going to put that money back into your purse and enjoy this cup of sinful delight." I grinned, bringing my finger to the tip of her nose.

Our eyes locked as she smiled shyly up at me. I looked at her and took her in—her soft, dark, silky hair, her striking blue eyes—and smiled as she bit her bottom lip. I did not know how my asshole friend could have done what he did to her. I look up when I heard a throat clear, and two cups were shoved in our direction. I took our drinks and held one cup for Tess to take. She took the cup, her fingers gently grazing mine. She brought the cup to her lips and took a sip of the rich, hot chocolate. Her eyes closed as she swallowed.

"My God, that is A-M-A-Z-I-N-G!" she exclaimed, her eyes lighting up as she looked at me.

I smiled. "I told you. You, um, have something right here," I said, lifting my fingers to the corner of my mouth. Her cheeks went pink as she quickly wiped at her mouth and looked up at me.

"That better?"

I chuckled. She'd missed the entire spot of chocolate, so I brought my thumb up to her lip and gently wiped away the smudge of chocolate that sat on the corner of her lip. "There," I said, smiling. "Let's continue, shall we." I placed my hand on the small of her back and guided her out into the mall.

The last couple of weeks, we had been spending an inordinate amount of time together. More than I think we'd ever had, and it was getting more difficult every day that passed not to let Derrick know we had been hanging out and that I was going to be going on the trip with her. I wasn't even sure why I wanted to tell him. Perhaps it was to make him angry. It certainly wasn't because I cared about what he thought. Tess whispered something to me, pointing at the shop across the way.

"Oh, and I want to go into the luggage shop. It's just around the corner here." She shoved her list into her purse. I followed her and, just as we'd stepped around the corner, Tess stopped outside the lingerie store and looked inside.

"Did you need to go in there for something?" I questioned. "If you do, I'll just grab a seat on the bench over there," I said, but then upon closer inspection, I noticed she was concentrating awfully hard on something inside the store.

"No," she whispered and shook her head, her bottom lip trembling.

I frowned and looked in the same direction she was. I couldn't believe my eyes. There inside was Derrick with Lucy. She had just gone into the changing room, and Derrick stood outside with a handful of lingerie. I looked back at Tess, who stood there, her eyes welling with tears as she watched the sickening display of affection going on in front of us.

"As if it wasn't bad enough…" she whispered. "All this does is pour salt into the wound." Then she bolted, running in the opposite direction and darting out the closest exit door.

I didn't know what to do. First, I watched as she ran outside, then I turned to watch as Lucy opened the changing room door and Derrick made some comment that made Lucy laugh. An anger filled me, one that I wasn't even familiar with, and I debated going in there and giving him a piece of my mind, but I didn't. Instead, I took off after Tess.

I ran out the exit door and looked toward my truck, but she was nowhere to be seen. I looked to my right and then my left, and that was where I spotted her, leaning up against the wall in the shadows, her back facing me. I could see her shoulders shake as she cried.

I approached her slowly and placed my hands on her shoulders, but she pulled away. "Don't, Maddox, please. Just leave me alone." She sniffled.

"Tess, please talk to me."

"Maddox, there is nothing to talk about. He cheated on me with her…with…"

"Lucy," I said, her name rolling off my tongue before I could stop myself.

Tess turned and looked up at me with tear-filled eyes. "You knew?" she exclaimed glaring at me, hurt filling her eyes. "How long has it been going on, Maddox?"

"It's not like that, Tess."

"How long, Maddox? How long have you known that he was screwing around on me?"

"I caught him eight months ago. I did what I could. I tried to talk to him, tried to talk sense into him, but he apparently didn't listen. He did what he wanted. In all honesty, I thought he'd stopped."

Tess paced back and forth, her body rigid. "Why the hell didn't you tell me?" she asked, pushing her hand into my chest. "If you knew, why didn't you say anything to me and save me all this...this embarrassment...this hurt?" Her tear-stained face broke my heart as she confronted me with the only question I didn't want to answer.

"I don't know, Tess. I put my trust in him when he begged me not to tell you, promising that he would stop. I know that isn't a good enough answer."

Just then the door to the mall opened and out stepped Derrick and Lucy, laughing, walking hand-in-hand across the parking lot as a lingerie bag hung from her hand. I watched as Tess turned back to me.

"He begged you not to. That is the most pathetic answer I have ever heard."

My heart sank. It wasn't my actual reason, but it was the one that was best fitting for now. Truth was I hadn't wanted to be the one to break her heart, and one day I would tell her the truth. I just couldn't bring myself to do it right now.

I went to place my hands on her shoulders, to comfort her, but instead she swung at me. I grabbed her arm, blocking the hit, as she fell into me. I wrapped my arms around her as she continued to try and fight, but the harder I held her, the quicker she exhausted herself, her body finally relaxing as she broke down into tears. She buried her head in my chest and cried. I stood there, my arms wrapped securely around her, and held her right there in the parking lot as tears poured from her eyes, followed by the sound of guttural sobs. I held her until her crying slowed, and finally, she just stood there resting against me.

"I'm sorry," she mumbled to me.

"No, I'm sorry. Sorry that I never told you. I know you're in pain and trust me when I tell you I know pain, Tess. I didn't want to be the one to do that to you. I didn't want to be the one that broke your heart," I admitted. I couldn't hold back the truth any longer. "I am so sorry that he did this to you."

"He didn't do this to me, Maddox. I did. And don't be sorry. This situation wasn't yours to tell. I'm sorry I got mad at you. This entire situation has just gutted me. I am sorry I took it out on you."

"It's okay, Tess. You can take it out on me. I have

strong shoulders," I whispered, pulling her against me and holding her tight. "You can take it out on me all you want, especially if it makes it easier for you."

"Could you take me home?"

I nodded and pressed a kiss to her forehead. I kept my arm wrapped around her shoulders and slipped the bags from her hand, then led her over to my truck. I opened the door for her, and she climbed into the passenger's seat and pulled the seatbelt across herself. Then she rested her head against the headrest and waited while I placed the bags in the backseat and walked around to the driver's side. We drove back to her place in silence, quiet music playing in the background.

By the time we pulled into her driveway she sat quietly with her eyes closed. I put the truck in park. "We're here."

She opened her eyes and looked up at the house for a moment, not saying anything, and then turned and looked at me and softly smiled. "You are a really great guy, Maddox. Thank you so much for being here."

"Of course. You going to be okay tonight?"

She nodded. "I think so. I'm going to go in, make a cup of tea, maybe watch a little TV, and then try and get some sleep."

"Okay, well, I am only a call away if you need me. I mean it, day or night."

"Thanks, but I will be fine." She climbed out of the

truck. and opened the back door, grabbing her bags. "I'll see you in a week?"

"I'll be here," I answered.

"Good night," she said, smiling at me behind her tears. She shut the door and sauntered up to the front door. I waited until she was safely inside, and then I backed out of the driveway and made my way home.

Tess

One Week Later

I shuffled through the dark house, carrying my mug of coffee and a plate of buttered toast into the living room. I was still in my pyjamas, and I sat down and turned on the TV. It was a little after midnight. Maddox would be here in two hours to pick me up to head to the airport.

I'd finished packing my bags last night, and I pulled my carry-on closer to me to quickly check the front pocket for all our travel documents. They sat there along with my passport and the money I had picked up at the bank earlier through the week. I had spent the entire week packing and repacking and had gone through my bag a dozen times to make sure I hadn't forgotten anything.

I took a bite of my toast, followed by a mouthful of coffee, when lights shone into the front window. I frowned, took another bite of my toast, and got up to glance out the window. It surprised me to see Maddox climbing out of his truck. "What the hell?" I mumbled to myself, closing the curtain and walking over to the front door, pulling it open as he walked up the walkway. "What are you doing here so early?"

"Couldn't sleep. Thought I'd come by and see if you were up yet."

"And if I wasn't?"

His eyes washed over me as he stepped inside the house, and a sexy smile appeared on his lips. "Well, I guess you would be getting up." He chuckled. "Little over-dressed for the plane, aren't you?"

I looked down at myself, my stretched-out T-shirt and dog ladened flannel pajama pants staring back up at me. "I just got up," I said, suddenly embarrassed by my sleep attire.

"I see. I thought we would get an early start. The weather's supposed to turn bad, and we have at least an hour's drive on good roads."

I stepped to the side so Maddox could come in and shut the door behind him. While he slipped off his coat and shoes, I couldn't help but take in the scent of his cologne. He smelled good enough to eat, but I shook my head to chase away that thought.

"Well, I guess I will run up and get dressed. Help yourself to coffee. I made extra, so we had enough for the road."

"Sounds good."

I watched as his large, muscular frame walked away from me and disappeared into the kitchen, where I heard him pull a mug from the cupboard. I smiled to myself. Maddox always thought ahead. I hadn't even thought about checking the weather.

"Thought you said you were heading up to shower?" I heard his deep voice behind me.

I jumped, turned, and smiled. He stood in the doorway to the dining room watching me. "I am. Thought you were getting coffee?"

"I did." He smiled, holding up a full mug.

Five hours later, we had boarded the plane. Maddox walked ahead of me down the aisle, my eyes firmly trained on his ass when he halted. I hadn't been paying attention and hadn't noticed that we were already at our seats. He lifted his bag above his head and slid it into the overhead carrier and turned to me.

"Did you want the window?" he questioned, stopping the entire line of people behind me from moving any further, instead of just sliding into the seat.

I shook my head. "No, you go ahead," I said, as the man behind me groaned at the fact that we were going to stand in the aisle and fight over the window seat.

"No, I insist. You take it." He grinned, waiting for me to climb in.

"No, Maddox, seriously, you take it," I insisted, but instead of climbing into the seat, he just stood there staring at me, a small smile on his lips.

"Would one of you take it. I've been up all night and would like to get settled so I can get some rest," the guy behind me gritted.

I stood there and looked at Maddox. Out of the both of us, he was the stubborn one, and I knew I probably didn't have a chance at winning with him. "I insist," he said, winking at me.

"Would you take the damn seat, sweetheart?" the man behind me snapped, shoving his bag into my back.

I winced in pain as he continued to shove. "Stop shoving me," I bit out, annoyed, as I turned to look at the man behind me.

"Then take the damn seat and flirt with him there instead of holding the rest of us up. Like I said, I was up all night."

I frowned and felt embarrassed at what the man behind me had suggested. I was not flirting with Maddox. I was about to say something when the man gave me another shove, causing me to fall forward into Maddox. He grabbed hold of me and held me steady for a moment. He let me go, and when I looked up, I saw Maddox was standing at his full height with his arms crossed over his chest. He had barely any head space left; he was intimidating at his full height of almost six feet, with his muscular chest puffed out. "Shove the lady again and you will ride in the overhead cargo area, because I'll put you there myself. Tess, take the seat," he demanded, nodding toward our seats.

As the men glared at one another, I slid into the seat in order to stop what I knew was sure to become a fight if the guy shoved Maddox. I shoved my bag under my seat, then turned toward Maddox, who still stood there looking down on the man.

"Maddox, sit down," I said under my breath, grabbing his hand and pulling him.

He slid into the seat beside me without taking his eyes off the man. The man glared at both of us as he walked by, grumbling under his breath. Once he was gone, we looked at one another and laughed.

"Are you going to catch any sleep on the flight?" he questioned.

I couldn't help but let out a yawn. "I sure hope so. What about you?"

"I'll try, but I don't trust that jackass," he said, laughing while he picked up the magazine in front of him and flipped through it, looking at the meal options. "You hungry?"

"A little."

"Tell me what you'd like, and I'll get it once they serve, in case you're asleep." He held the book down so we could both look through it and flipped the pages slowly, giving me the chance to decide.

"Just get me the oatmeal and maybe some fruit."

"Oatmeal and fruit, got it."

I could feel my stomach aching once they started going over the safety procedures of the plane while we began slowly making our way out to the runway. I hated everything there was about flying. Derrick normally held my hand when we took off, when we landed, and if there was any moment of turbulence. I had hoped to be asleep by the time we took off.

As the plane started speeding up, I looked over to Maddox, who sat relaxed in his seat with his eyes closed. I prayed he didn't notice that I was gripping the armrest so tightly that my knuckles were turning white. I leaned back against my seat and closed my eyes as the plane sped up even faster.

I was trying so hard to stay inside my head that I never heard Maddox speak to me. Instead, I felt a slight tap on my arm. I opened my eyes to see him watching me intently, a smirk on his face. "Are you okay? You look a little pale."

I shook my head. "Yep."

"Then why does it look like you are going to throw up?" He chuckled.

"Okay, I hate flying."

Maddox chuckled. "You hate flying, and yet you booked a trip to Paris?"

I nodded. "I've always wanted to see it," I said, closing my eyes even tighter than before as the plane accelerated even faster. I hated the feeling of the pressure on my body.

He was quiet, and it felt like an eternity as the pressure built up on my body. I could feel the panic rising in me when I felt his warm hand on mine as he pried my fingers loose from the armrest. I opened my eyes and looked down as he slipped his hand into mine. "Squeeze all you want."

I swallowed hard. "What if I hurt you?" I questioned.

"You won't, go ahead," he said, meeting my eyes.

He had the most intense blue eyes I had ever seen, and the longer I stared into them, the less I thought about where I was and what was actually going on around us. It felt like minutes had passed as we sat there looking into one another eyes, my hand in his, and then he smiled.

"You can let go. We are in the air now."

I blinked and looked over out the window to see we were already up and in the air and I had barely even noticed the takeoff. I looked back at him, shyly smiled, and released his hand. "Thank you. That wasn't so bad at all."

"Oatmeal and fruit, right? Coffee?"

"Yes, please." I nodded. "Think I am going to try and get some rest," I said, sitting back in my seat and placing my headphones into my ears.

I adjusted myself and snuggled into something warm. Then I felt a jostling and opened my eyes. I stayed where I was for a few moments, breathing in a cologne I absolutely loved. Then I felt a heavy object on my shoulder. I raised my head and looked around the plane. We'd been in the air for a few hours and most people were asleep. I felt the plane shake—turbulence. The ding of the seatbelt sign caused me to panic. I looked down at my hand; it rested on Maddox's chest, and then I felt his hand grip my shoulder. He had wrapped his arm around me while I had slept.

"What is it? What's wrong?" I heard his deep voice murmur.

I sat up, pulling at the wrap I had wrapped around me earlier. "My God, I'm sorry. I must have fallen asleep."

"It's all good, Tess, not a problem. I was trying to catch a few winks myself," he whispered, shifting in his seat.

The plane dropped and shook, and instantly I panicked, jumping closer to him. He let out a throaty chuckle again, and I realized what I was doing and tried to compose myself and stop panicking.

"Relax, would you?"

"I'm fine. I'll just be happier when we land." I giggled nervously, sitting back in my seat, panicking silently.

"Come here," he whispered, pulling me into his side once again. "There is no need to panic. You're perfectly safe here."

I never thought the plane ride would end. We'd spent the last forty minutes of our flight experiencing massive turbulence, but all I could concentrate on was his words to me, *'you're perfectly safe here.'* We'd finally arrived at the hotel, and now, we both followed the bellhop down the hall to what would be our room.

"You'll need to jiggle the key a little," he said as he wiggled it in the lock before turning the key, then he turned, smiled at us, and turned the key, the lock clicking. He opened the door, and we followed him in. I glanced around the room. A bottle of champaign sat cooling in an ice bucket, a card that read *Congratulations to the Newly Married Couple* sat beside it.

"Welcome, Mr. and Mrs. Wright. Could I pour you both a glass of champagne?" the bellhop offered, walking over and pulling the bottle from the ice, while waiting for a signal from Maddox.

I felt my face fall as I looked around the room, spotting his-and-her robes laying on the bottom of the bed. All of this had been part of the upgrade that I had forgotten to cancel. Maddox took one look at me, and then cleared his throat, stepping forward.

"Thank you, sir, but I'm sure you can understand that we have both had an extremely long flight," Maddox said once again, looking over at me.

"Perhaps a nice hot bath? I'd be more than happy to send someone up to draw it for you. There is a tub for two," he said, heading over to what I figured was the bathroom.

I could feel the tears sting my eyes, trying to figure out why the hell I had come on this trip. I did not know that this was going to be so hard. Instead of standing there waiting for the tears to fall, I walked over and opened the curtains, looking down on the streets below us, trying hard to divert my thoughts.

"Honestly, sir, I thank you, but I just really want to spend some time alone with my love. If you catch my drift."

I turned in time to see Maddox shove some money toward the man and lead him over to the door, trying his best to get rid of him.

"Certainly, sir," he whispered, finally stepping into the hall in time for Maddox to shut and lock the door. He turned to look in my direction, while I stood there staring at everything that reminded me of what this trip was supposed to be.

I didn't know if it was the fact that I was exhausted,

emotionally drained, or what, but my hand went up to cover my mouth to stop the sobs that were threatening to escape, but they won, and my shoulders began to shake.

"Oh, Tess," I heard Maddox murmur as he walked over to where I stood. "I'm sorry, sweetie."

I didn't fight it this time. I turned to him and buried myself into the comfort of his arms.

Maddox

We stood in the room, her face buried in my chest, the only sound were her sobs as tears poured. The only thing I knew to do was to comfort her the best I could. So, I held her small frame tightly against mine and let her cry.

"I'm sorry, Maddox." She sniffled. "I didn't expect this to be so hard, and then the bellhop thought you were my...my...husband...it just...humiliating." She cried as she buried her face in my chest yet again as more tears fell.

"Tess, it's fine. Really, he doesn't know, and it's not like I'm bothered by it," I said, placing my finger under her chin, tilting her head back so she could meet my eyes.

She wiped the tears from her cheeks. "How can it not bother you?"

"Look at me, do I look bothered by it?" I questioned.

"But I didn't remove the upgrade package. I didn't

even change the suite, and now we only have a king-size bed. I certainly didn't think this through." She sniffled, looking over her shoulder at the bed that sat behind us. "This is nothing but a disaster. Now I am going to be even more humiliated when I ask the front desk to change our room to one with two queen beds." She cried, pulling away from me and sitting down on the bottom of the bed, picking up the robe that sat there, running her finger over the embroidered letters.

I reached down and removed the monogrammed robe from her hands. "So what, so I sleep on the couch. I can call down for an extra blanket and pillow. It looks comfortable enough," I said, throwing the robe down on the desk and walking over to the couch, lying on it. "Yep, totally comfortable," I said. "It will be fine."

That couch could have been as hard as concrete, and I would have told her I'd sleep on it because she was literally breaking my heart standing there with those beautiful eyes of hers filled with tears.

"Really?" she questioned, her voice shaky.

"Really. Now it has been a long day of travel. Why don't I go in and run you a hot bubble bath in that gigantic tub in there, and you can soak and decompress while I order us some food. Then you can lie down and have a long-ass nap, and we can get this adventure on the road tomorrow."

"No, Maddox, really, I'll be fine. See, fine," she said,

wiping away the tears from her cheeks and looking at me with tired, red, bloodshot eyes.

I studied her for a minute and noticed the tremble in her bottom lip. I could see she was about to break down again any second as her eyes landed back on the bathrobes. I shook my head. "Nope, I insist."

I made my way into the bathroom and turned on the water. She came in just as I held my hand under the water to check the temperature as steam rose. She leaned against the wall, exhausted, as she watched me reach for a bottle on the counter. I dumped some of it into the bath, bubbles instantly forming.

"You don't need to do this," she murmured behind me.

"I know, but I am. Now, let this fill. I am going to leave you alone. I want you to relax. What bag did you put that book in. You know, the one you bought at the airport?"

"My carry-on. Why?"

I held my finger up and took off into the other room and found the book sticking out of the bag. Grabbing it, I made my way back into the bathroom. "Here you are." I smiled, holding up the book. "Now relax," I said, stepping forward, placing my hand at the back of her neck, pulling her forward, and placing a kiss on her forehead. I slowly backed up and pulled the door closed, but before it clicked shut, I heard her call my name.

"Maddox?"

"Yeah?"

"Thank you," she whispered, her voice crackling.

"My pleasure, Tess. Enjoy." I smiled and then pulled the door shut and turned around to look around at the room.

As I walked over to my bag, everything I passed reminded me she was supposed to be here on her honeymoon. I couldn't allow her to walk out of that bathroom to see all that again. So instead of unpacking, I took a few minutes and removed everything that would remind her of that fact, including the his-and-hers robes from the end of the bed, all while cursing Derrick under my breath.

My best friend had done this to her, ripped her heart out and broke it into a million little pieces, all because he couldn't resist temptation. The more I thought about it, the angrier I got. I knew what loss felt like, and I would never do this to someone intentionally. I never wanted anything to ever make me feel that way again, nor would I ever take for granted the person I chose in the future to spend my life with, like he had.

As I looked around, my eyes landed to the card sitting beside the champaign. I walked over and ripped it into pieces, depositing it into the garbage, and then took one more look around the room, making sure I had gotten everything that might set her off again. Satisfied I had taken care of everything, I went to unpack my bags but stopped. I'd promised her something to eat, so I took a few minutes, sat down, and went through the room service menu. The second I had decided on something, I picked up the phone and placed the order, then began unpacking my bag.

The end of *White Christmas* played on the television while I listened to Tess softly breathing. Night was falling, and the room was getting darker, but she still slept. As the credits rolled, I reached for the remote and was about to change the channel when she rolled over and stretched.

"What time is it?" she asked in a sleepy voice.

"Almost six," I answered, checking my watch.

"Oh...," she said, sitting up and looking around the room. "Why didn't you wake me up. I slept the entire day away."

"You needed your rest." I shrugged. "I'd be lying if I said I didn't nap as well."

"Yeah, but you didn't sleep the entire day away, did you?" she asked, kicking off the covers and sitting up on the edge of the bed. She ran her fingers through her messed-up hair and let out a yawn. "We should get out, take a walk, and maybe get some food. You're probably starving."

I chuckled. "Well, the hotel apparently booked us in for dinner downstairs in the restaurant at seven thirty," I said, getting up and grabbing the reminder card that someone had slid under the door while we'd been sleeping. I held it up for her to see.

"Oh God, I forgot all about that. We don't have to eat there. That was Derrick's idea. He was the one who secured the meal with his credit card."

I sat up, keenly interested, and leaned forward, resting my forearms on my thighs. "Is that so?"

"Yes, he didn't think we would want to go out on our first night here. Or perhaps he just didn't want to take me out." She shrugged.

"I see. Well, that was big of him, wasn't it?" I gave her a crooked smile. "Before we decide on where we are eating, I want to make one rule for the rest of this trip."

"What's that?"

"I don't want to hear his name leave your lips again. You can call him anything you want, except his name."

Tess let out a little laugh and shook her head. "You are too much."

"I may be, but he upset you, and even though he is my best friend, he has downright pissed me off. So, from now moving forward, his name does not leave your lips. Now, get up and get yourself dressed."

"What for? Where are we going?" she questioned, looking down at her herself. "Let's just order in room service or something from a restaurant close by," she insisted.

I shook my head and held up the invitation and threw it over by where she sat on the bed, a grin on my face. "Nope, we are going to enjoy a dinner on that bastard. You said his credit card holds the reservation right, so..."

Tess let out an adorable giggle and buried her face in her hands. I couldn't help but smile. I loved hearing her laugh.

"Listen, I'm going to hit that shower," I said, getting up and making my way into the bathroom. "Get yourself dressed." I winked as I walked past her, shutting the door.

I'd realized as I shaved I'd left my clothes hanging in the closet, so I splashed some cologne on my neck and wrapped a towel securely around my waist and opened the bathroom door. Tess was sitting at the desk writing something down, her back to me.

"Bathroom is free," I said, expecting her to get up and go in as I made my way over to the closet where I'd hung most of my clothes.

"Great," she mumbled, not paying any attention to me.

I pulled my dress pants and a shirt from the hanger and turned around, expecting her to be gone. However, she sat there, her cheeks slightly flushed, her eyes running over my body, finally landing on the knot at the side of the towel. Her eyes travelled back up my body and she bit her lower lip. She met my eyes and noticed I'd been watching her. She cleared her throat, and got up nervously, walking over to her bag. "Great, um, I'll just be a few minutes."

"Take your time."

She grabbed the dress that lay at the foot of the bed and her bag and, without looking at me again, made her way into the bathroom, shutting the door behind her.

Tess

I took a moment and leaned against the cold wooden door of the bathroom. Maddox was right, Derrick was history, and I needed to stop mentioning him. I closed my eyes and took a deep, cleansing breath and, in that moment, the scent of his cologne filled my nostrils as I tried hard to put what I had just seen out of my mind. His strong shoulders, that wide chest, those rock-hard abs, and that spattering of hair that led down, way down below the towel that wrapped around his waist. *Derrick was history.*

"Stop it, Tess," I whispered to myself. "You're only six weeks out of a relationship, and you're just feeling lonely because it's Christmas and because you're looking for a way to get back at Derrick." Yet, when I closed my eyes again, the only thing I saw was Maddox, standing there in that white towel, looking deliciously sexy, his blue eyes focused on me.

I shook the vision from my head and walked over to the mirror and fixed my hair, quickly doing my makeup. I picked up the dress I'd placed on the counter, quickly sliding into it, and looked at myself in the mirror. I smoothed the sides of the green silky fabric over my curves, and then stood back and looked at myself in the mirror. I'd purchased this dress strictly for this trip, and at the time, I had loved how the fabric clung to my body. Now it did nothing but make me feel self-conscious. I let out a sigh. It would have to do, I thought to myself, then I slipped my feet into my black heels, turned, and looked at myself once again, trying to find the courage to open that bathroom door.

You look fine. Now enjoy dinner and forget about it all. I let out a breath, ran my hand over the sides of the dress once again, turned, and pulled the door open and stepped into the room.

My eyes moved instantly to Maddox, who stood with his back to me. He looked different as he stood before me wearing dark dress pants and a white dress shirt. He turned around and stopped buttoning his shirt, his eyes lingering on me.

"Wow," he whispered under his breath, his eyes dancing over me as he swallowed hard.

"What?" I asked, looking down at myself for fear

something was out of place.

"Tess, you look...gorgeous."

I could feel my face heat at his words. I wasn't used to compliments; Derrick never handed them out. "Thank you, but..."

He held up his hands, stopping me from saying any more. "I mean it, Tess, you look amazing." He walked over, his eyes glued to me, and took my hand, spinning me around.

"Thank you. You look good yourself," I replied, our eyes locked as something unsaid passed between us. "We should get going." I glanced to the clock, trying to shake off the uncomfortable feeling I could only describe as attraction.

"Let's, shall we," he said while he finished buttoning his shirt before reaching for his wallet and the room key from the small desk. His eyes washed over me once more before he pulled the room door open. He held the door for me while I walked into the hallway, and together, we made our way down to the restaurant.

I sat listening with my undivided attention as Maddox finished his story during dinner. It was refreshing listening to him. He was so different from Derrick. His stories were entertaining, funny, and he answered every question I had, never getting annoyed that I had interrupted him.

"...and that is how I decided to become a firefighter," Maddox said, sitting back against his chair, picking up his wineglass and emptying it.

"I can't believe you've never told me that story before." I smiled.

"I guess the chance to tell it never came up. We've never had a lot of alone time together, to be honest." He shrugged, picking up the dessert menu that sat on the table beside him, flipping through the pages.

"I think I am going to pass on desert." I yawned, sitting back against my chair. I was stuffed from dinner.

"No way. I will not let you miss out on the best part of the meal," Maddox objected, shaking his head. "Plus, it's Paris. I've heard from some guys at work that they have the best desserts here."

"Oh God, I have to pass. There is no way anything more is going to fit in this dress." I giggled.

"Then I guess we will just sit here and wait until it will." He winked and continued to look over the choices. "I think we should have the crème brûlée."

I crinkled my nose. "Really?"

"Yes, why?"

"I don't..."

"Don't you dare tell me you don't like it. You've never tried it here. It is apparently one of the top ten desserts in

Paris, and besides, that garbage we get back home isn't crème brûlée."

I couldn't help but laugh. "How do you know what the top ten desserts are here?"

He shrugged. "I might have been bored this afternoon, and hungry, so I did a little research while you were sleeping."

I couldn't help but smile as he sat there staring back at me. Those eyes, his smile, his persistence, everything about him suddenly made me very happy.

"All right, fine, I guess I will try it," I said, giving up.

"Perfect." He nodded, closing the menu and waving to our server.

With dessert ordered and coffee in front of us, I finally decided to ask him the question that I'd been dying to ask since I had met him. He had just returned from the washroom and had sat down when I cleared my throat. "Can I ask you something?"

"Of course?" he said, gazing at me. "I'm an open book."

"Ever since I've known you, I've never heard you ever talk of a girlfriend. I can't even imagine why you are single."

Maddox turned and looked over his shoulder, shifting uncomfortably in his seat. I figured I had perhaps crossed a line with him and abruptly stopped my question.

"Never mind, you don't need to answer. It's none of

my business. Sorry if I made you uncomfortable."

"I'm not uncomfortable, Tess. I just figured Der...I mean that the asshole would have told you," he said, shifting again in his seat.

"Oh. I'd asked him a couple of times, but no, he didn't, but forget I asked. What time did you say you were heading out tomorrow?" I questioned, trying to change the subject, but instead of answering my question, he surprised me by taking a deep breath and looking me directly in the eyes.

"I was engaged to be married eight years ago. Jenn and I dated in high school, but life separated us shortly before college. We reconnected when she moved back to town and began to work at the fire station. It had been years since we had seen one another, but things between us heated up pretty fast once we had reconnected. We were so in love, and I'd asked her to marry me six months later. We had set the date for a year and a half later. She was so excited, and soon we were in crazy planning stages for the wedding. It had been about four months when she came home from a doctor's appointment and told me she was pregnant. Of course, my mind spun, we hadn't talked about having a family yet. Hell, at the time, I didn't even know if I wanted kids. Yet the longer I allowed the idea to grow on me, I became more and more excited. She finally talked me into moving the wedding date up because she didn't want to be showing or carrying a baby in her arms at the wedding, so we stopped all the planning and agreed to elope. We'd booked our trip and had one month left before the big day."

"Anyway, as time passed, she began having minor complications with her pregnancy because of the job and all the heavy lifting. Her doctor had wanted her to immediately stop actively fighting fires and have her put on desk duty, but she was stubborn, she loved her job. Desk duty would also mean that we wouldn't have been able to fly away. Instead, she convinced the doctor that she would go off right after our wedding, and so she agreed. One week before our trip, she had picked up a shift. She called me on her dinner break, and that was when the call came in. A bunch of teenagers were out partying at some abandoned barn in the country and a fire had broken out. There were three teenagers trapped inside."

He grew quiet, swallowed hard, then picked up his glass and drank down the last of his wine. I studied his face and was sure I caught a glimpse of a tear, but I said nothing. I just kept my attention focused on Maddox, waiting for him to continue.

"She was part of the search and rescue team, and she went to look for those kids. She went in and spotted the kids on the upper level. The barn, under normal conditions, wasn't safe enough to be in, never mind at this point because the fire had compromised any of the structural integrity of the building that it may have had left. Instead, she did what they trained her to do. She went up after them. Anyway, she climbed the steps and had taken about five steps on the upper floor, and that was when the floor gave way. What no one knew was that the barn had a ten-foot foundation under the main floor, so when she fell, she didn't just fall one floor, but broke right through the main floor and landed on the foundation floor." He finished, wiping at his eyes.

"Oh, Maddox, I had no idea," I whispered, bringing my hand to my heart, my eyes filling with tears.

"She died instantly, broken neck and back. There was nothing anyone could have done." He was quiet for a moment as he stared down at the table. "You know, I wasn't lying to you when I told you I knew what pain was," he stated, meeting my eyes.

"How did you ever move on from that?"

"Lots of therapy." He chuckled. "However, to be honest with you, what helped the most was time."

"Time?" I repeated.

He nodded. "Time has a way of healing all things. It certainly doesn't feel like it at the moment, and it's not like it never bothers me anymore or that she doesn't enter my mind, but I can promise you it gets easier the more time passes by. Time heals everything. Of course, it all depends on the depth of the wound that was created and how long you let it affect you. Some things take way longer, obviously, than others, and then there are situations and events that, at the time, you feel like you'll never get over, but after a couple of weeks, you barely think of them."

I gave thought to what he had said and watched as he dug his spoon into his dessert.

"Now I feel totally silly going on and on over something like this, after hearing what you went through." Maddox always had a way of putting things into perspective, and I saw why now; he had grown up way faster than his years. "Thank you for sharing your story with me. I'm sorry if it was hard for you to talk about."

"It's not hard anymore. There was a time that I wouldn't have been able to. Like I said, time heals. Don't let my story discount how you feel. Everyone is different when it comes to how bad something affects them. However, I'm going to hedge a guess and say that you'll be back to your old self by the end of this trip," He said, his voice full of confidence, as he met my eyes.

"How can you be so sure?"

"I'd say with the few weeks it's been already has added healing time. Plus, for the next ten days, you just need to lose yourself in your surroundings. You are, after all, in one of the most beautiful cities with amazing food. Plus, you have amazing company, if I say so myself. This time, right here and now, is your time to heal."

I nodded, giving thought to what he was saying. "I just don't know how you can be so sure?"

"Tess, guys like Derrick don't deserve women like you.

They have no concept of what it is they are giving up. They don't understand what it means to value someone. He doesn't have a care in the world about that, because he's never been on the receiving end. He has just moved girl to girl whenever the moment suited him. He certainly deserves none of your tears, none of your sadness, because a real man wouldn't have put you in this position to begin with. Instead, they'd sit in front of you and tell you that they didn't feel things were working out before they ever decided to bed someone else."

My heart skipped a beat at his words, and when I blinked, a tear slid down my cheek. I quickly reached up and wiped it away. "Thank you so much for being here."

"Now, no more tears. What you really need to do is dig into this dessert because it's fucking amazing," he said, winking, as he placed his spoon in his mouth.

I grabbed my spoon and slowly dug into the rich, creamy dessert and slid it into my mouth. He was right, it was the most amazing thing I had ever tasted, and I didn't even like crème brûlée. I had just scraped the last of my little bowl when Maddox cleared his throat.

"I got you something," he said, reaching down beside his chair and bringing up a small box wrapped in shiny gold paper.

"What is that?" I asked. "I never saw you bring anything down."

"That's because it was hidden." He held the box out

for me to take.

I quickly unwrapped the gold foil paper and opened the box. Inside was a silver picture frame with the picture of us I had taken of us in the airport before we boarded the plane. "How did you do this?"

He shrugged. "Guess you could say I was a busy guy while you were sleeping the day away."

My heart felt full as I stared down at the picture of us. Then I looked up to Maddox, who sat there watching me, a smile on his face with a look that I hoped I'd never forget.

We took our time walking back to our room after dinner, walking through the lobby of the hotel, looking in a couple of little shops. We finally made our way back up to the room. I went to put the key in the lock, but Maddox stopped me. "Let me," he said, reaching for the key in my hand. "I have a little surprise for you."

"Another one?" I questioned, not letting go of the key.

His hand grazed mine as he gently removed the key from my fingers and his eyes met mine. "Yes, another one," he whispered, jiggling the key like the bellhop had shown us and unlocking the door.

"Now just wait," he said. "Cover your eyes."

I did as he told me, covering my eyes as I listened to door squeak as he pushed it open. He stood only inches behind me, and I could feel the warmth radiating off his body. The scent of his skin combined with the scent of his cologne sent waves through me.

"I've got you. Now step forward," he whispered, sliding his arm around me placing his hand on my abdomen, his warm breath tickling my ear. I could feel my skin already pebbling as I took the first step forward. "I have the door, go ahead."

I took a few steps forward into our room and heard the door close behind us. "You can open them now," He said.

I blinked, allowing my eyes to focus, and right in front of me stood a gorgeously decorated Christmas tree. "Oh my, how—how did you do this?" I asked, turning to look at him.

He shrugged. "I know how much you love Christmas. Your house is always so beautifully decorated, so I had this done while we had dinner. The hotel was more than accommodating. After all, we are newlyweds." He winked, causing me to laugh. "Can't blame a guy for using that to his advantage, can you?"

I shook my head and wandered over to the tree, looking at the all the decorations, and couldn't help but feel emotional. He had done this for me. Instantly, I walked over to him and wrapped my arms around his neck, pressing myself into him for a hug. "Thank you so much. Even though we had a rocky start, this trip is turning out to be so wonderful." I smiled, kissing his cheek.

"You're welcome, Tess," he murmured, wrapping his muscular arms around me.

A little while later, Maddox had gone down to the small store that was off the main lobby, and I stood out on the balcony overlooking the city. I quickly dialled my mom's number and waited for her to answer. Finally, on the fifth ring, she picked up.

"Hey, honey, how is everything? Are you enjoying your trip?"

"Hey, Mom, everything is going well."

"I'm so happy to hear that. The flight was okay? I know how much you hate flying."

I giggled, thinking back to it. "Yes, it was good. I had a good flying partner. So, it helped."

"Glad to hear that. I want you to have the best time while you're away."

I thought back to dinner and Maddox's story and realized he had been right, that this was the time that I needed to live because Derrick deserved none of my tears. "I'm going to go, Mom. I love you and just wanted to let you know everything is fine."

"I'm so glad to hear that. Love you, too, sweetie. Now go off and enjoy Paris."

Maddox

I stood under the spray of the shower, allowing the hot water time to warm my body. We'd spent the day shopping on our own and had met back at the room a little after five to get ready for a night out on the town. I had booked us dinner reservations at a little local restaurant for seven thirty while I'd been out and had called Tess immediately after telling her I'd found a place. I closed my eyes, stood against the wall, and let the water run over me.

"Maddox, are you okay if I come in and grab my makeup bag? I left it on the counter by accident and I need it," I heard Tess call. When I didn't respond right away, she continued, "I promise I won't look." She giggled.

"It's fine, Tess, go ahead." I chuckled.

I could barely make out her form through the fogged shower glass. Instead I watched her shadow as she quickly made her way to the counter. She grabbed her bag and took off into the room, closing the door behind her. I laughed to myself at how fast she'd left the room. She acted like she'd never been in a bathroom with a naked man before.

I took one final rinse, then shut the water off and stepped out of the shower and was reaching for a towel when the door opened again, only I didn't have time to grab it and wrap it around myself. It was too late. Tess already had seen everything I had to offer.

"Oh my God! I'm so sorry! I thought you were in the shower still!" she exclaimed, covering her eyes.

I cleared my throat and turned to look at her over my shoulder. She stood there in nothing but her bra and panties, her hands over her eyes, her cheeks flushed. I pulled the towel off the hook and covered my semi-hard cock, taking a minute to allow my eyes to wander down her bra and panty-clad body. I could feel my cock hardening in my hand as I continued to look at her. I loved the way the black lace bra and panties looked against her creamy flesh. "It's okay."

"No, it's not. My God. I'm so embarrassed," she cried, turning, and running back out into the room, pulling the door shut behind her.

I stood there for a few moments, my hard cock in my hand, gripping it as it throbbed. I blew out a breath and turned the water back on, climbing back in under the cold water, and chuckled to myself. Her cheeks were so red, and she'd left so fast that I'd barely had enough time to say anything.

I stepped out of the bathroom half an hour later, dressed in jeans and a sweater. My eyes instantly landed on Tess. She stood before me in a gorgeous red dress, similar to the one she had on the night before, yet all I could picture was her standing before me in the matching red-and-black bra and panty set, she'd had on.

"Maddox, I'm so sorry," she said instantly. "I really thought you were still in the shower. I never would have come in knowing you..." Her cheeks flamed red again.

"It's fine, Tess. I don't think I have anything you haven't seen before." I winked, trying to take a bit of tension out of the room.

I adored how quickly she hid her eyes from me, her cheeks still red with embarrassment.

"Like I said, I'm sorry. I'm never going to be able to look at you again."

I chuckled. "Of course you will, it's fine," I repeated, moving over to her and tapping her nose with my forefinger, trying to make her feel at ease. "Now let's head out, shall we."

She dropped her hands and looked up at me.

"See, that wasn't so hard, was it?" I said in a low voice, studying her eyes.

She shook her head. "No," she murmured and reached

for the red shawl that lay on the end of the bed and wrapped it around her shoulders.

I grabbed my jacket and held the door open for her. We walked in silence down the hall to the elevator. When we hit the lobby, I placed my hand on the small of her back, guiding her out into the street, and grabbed a cab.

The restaurant wasn't that far from the hotel, and we were there rather quickly. We sat in the front window looking out onto the softly lit side street, looking over our menus in silence.

I couldn't help but occasionally glance up. She sat across from me, biting her thumb innocently as she looked over the menu. I couldn't stop my mind from drifting to her standing in that bathroom, her full breasts spilling over the top of her bra. She looked good enough to eat for dinner, and the longer I watched her, the more I could feel myself growing aroused at the thought.

She glanced up and caught me watching her. "What is it?" she questioned, closing the menu and looking out at the lightly snow-covered street.

"Know what you're having?" I asked.

"The chicken. What about you?"

"The same. Thought we would start off with a charcuterie board, or perhaps the olive tapenade."

"Either would be fine with me, so your choice."

"All right then."

"And wine," we both said in unison as we looked

across at one another. There was definitely a tension between us that hadn't been there before.

Once the food had been delivered and the wine had started flowing, the tension dropped between us, the conversation never stopping. She told me all about her day shopping, the things she had seen and some things she had purchased. I shared with her all about my day, told her about the ski shop I had found. The more I talked about it, I was sure I almost had her convinced to take lessons once we got to the skiing part of our trip.

She sat across from me, running her fingers around the rim of her wine glass, her eyes glued to mine as I spoke. Yet when I brought up the offer of teaching her to ski again, she shook her head no.

"Seriously, I'm a disaster on two feet. I don't want to end up in a body cast." She laughed as she took the last sip of her wine.

My eyes ran from her eyes to her lips and back again. "Do you honestly think I'd let that happen?" I questioned as I slipped my credit card into the billfold.

"What are you doing?" she asked, reaching for the billfold I'd placed on the edge of the table.

"Uh, what does it look like?" I said, picking it back up and handing it to the server who'd appeared at the perfect time.

"Maddox, you're not paying for dinner!" she exclaimed quietly, leaning forward in her seat.

"Oh but I am. She already took my card." I laughed. "Now, seriously, do you really think I would let you get hurt out on the hills?" I questioned.

She shook her head, looking rather bothered at the fact that I insisted on paying for dinner. "No, I know you wouldn't," she answered as I filled her glass with the last of the wine.

"Then what is the problem?" I asked, picking up my empty glass and holding it up in a mock cheer, smiling at her.

We stepped out onto the sidewalk, and I went to hail a cab, but Tess grabbed my arm, stopping me. "How about we walk back?"

Snow was gently falling from the sky, then I looked over at her, down to her heels, and shook my head. "Tess, you aren't exactly dressed for an evening stroll in the cold and snow."

"I'll be fine. I had all that wine. Plus, it's so pretty with the snow falling," she said, holding her hand up to catch the falling flakes. "Please?"

"It is beautiful," I said, complimenting her more than our surroundings. "I guess we can walk back. Just be careful okay," I said quietly, looking around at the empty street, testing the sidewalks to see if they were slippery.

"I will be."

We'd taken a couple of steps when Tess stepped on a patch of ice and went flying. I scrambled to catch her before she went down, and wrapped my arms around her waist just in time. She let out a scream followed by a laugh. "Stupid ice," she muttered.

"Are you okay?" I asked, standing her up and steadying her.

"Yeah, I'm good. Now you don't have to wonder why I won't ski."

"Yeah, but I caught you, didn't I."

"You did, so I guess you were right. You probably wouldn't let anything happen to me on that hill." She laughed.

"I told you," I answered, winking at her, making sure she was steady on her feet before releasing my grip on her.

She was just about to take a step forward when I held my arm out for her to take, which she wrapped hers through and held onto. Words seemed to stop flowing as we walked through the streets. We'd only gotten to the end of the block when I felt her shiver against me.

"Here," I said, stopping, removing my jacket.

"No, you need that. Don't be silly. I'm fine. I just need to adjust my shall." I watched as she pulled it around herself a little tighter.

"That flimsy thing? Tess, I'm fine," I insisted, holding the jacket open, waiting for her to slide into it as she shivered again.

She looked up at me but didn't argue. She rubbed her arms before sliding one arm and then the next into my coat, wrapping it around her. Then she slid her arm through mine and we continued our walk back to the hotel. She surprised me when she rested her head against my shoulder as we walked. If I were being honest with myself, I didn't want the night to end, and it didn't seem to take long and we were walking into the lobby of our hotel. "Did you want any more wine?" I asked before we approached the elevator.

She innocently shook her head in a yes motion, and I held my finger up and made my way to the front desk, asking them to have one delivered to the room. Then I made my way back over to Tess just in time for the elevator door to open.

The wine had gone down way too fast, and the bottle now sat empty on the desk. Tess lay on the bed, and I sat on the couch, a movie playing on the TV.

"I'm freezing," she muttered, her teeth chattering as she crawled under the covers. "How can you sit there like that? Aren't you cold?" she questioned as I looked down at myself in nothing but boxers, the blanket I used the night before curled in a ball at my feet.

"I'm good," I replied, downing the rest of my wine. "I'm like a human furnace."

"Well, if you're like a furnace, why don't you come over here and warm me up?" She giggled as a hiccup escaped her lips.

As much as I wanted to hear that invite, she'd had too much to drink, and I knew it was the alcohol talking, so I shook my head and relaxed back on the couch. "You'll warm up under those blankets soon enough," I said, feeling my cock jerk as my mind wandered back to the bathroom incident this afternoon.

"Please," she whined, "I'm frozen. I may even have frostbite." She giggled, holding up her fingers and wiggling them back and forth.

I couldn't help but smile. She was way too cute. I let out a breath. "Ten minutes, Tess, that's it," I said, getting up off the couch and moving over to empty side of the bed. Ten minutes would be all I could handle lying beside her. I was about to lie down on top of the covers when she looked up at me.

"What are you doing?" She asked, with innocent eyes.

"What you asked. Warming you up," I stated, looking down at her. There was a playful glint in her eyes as she stared up at me.

"You can't warm me up if you're on top of the covers." She giggled, reaching over and pulling the blankets down to expose the sheets, her bare leg sticking out from under the blankets. "Just crawl under the covers and shut the lights off. They are bright and hurting my eyes."

I did not have a clue at what I was doing by crawling into bed with her even if it was only to warm her up, but I reached under the lamp anyways and killed the lights. The room was now bathed in the soft glow from the TV and the tree. I had barely crawled under the covers when Tess moved into my side, pressing her body up against mine.

"That is so much better," she whispered more to herself than me as she wrapped her arm around my waist, placing one leg on top of mine. "So much better," she whispered again, a hiccup escaping her as she closed her eyes.

Tension filled my body as I felt her press herself against me. I placed my arm under her head, pulling her frozen body tighter against mine. My heart pounded in my chest as I relaxed back against the pillow and placed one arm behind my head. There was no way I should be in this position, I thought to myself as I focused my attention on the TV, trying to ignore the ache I felt building in my cock as she fell asleep in my arms.

Tess

The instant I opened my eyes, pain seared through my head. The bright-green numbers on the alarm clock pierced my eyes.

I rubbed them and blinked. It was only five forty-five; the room was still dark. I could hear sleet hitting the window, and I snuggled farther down under the warm covers, trying hard to ignore the pounding headache I'd achieved from drinking too much wine. I could hear a soft snore coming from Maddox. I went to roll over to lie on my back to see if that helped the headache when I felt slight movement behind me, followed by the slight puff of breath on my shoulder.

I raised my head up and looked over at the couch where Maddox normally slept. It was empty, the throw pillows strewn about. His blanket lay in a heap at the end of the couch. I brought my hand out and placed it on top of the covers and looked over my shoulder, then I lay my head back down on the pillow as panic filled me. Why the hell was Maddox in bed with me?

I tried to think back to last night. We'd walked back to the hotel, and got more wine downstairs, and came back to the room. The rest was a total blur. I glanced over at the desk and could see the outline of a wine bottle. *What the hell happened?*

I was about to get up when Maddox let out a low grumble, his arm wrapping around my waist as he pulled himself into me, so we were now even closer than before.

Oh my God, had we slept together? The panic I was feeling filled me even more as I tried hard to remember what had gone on last night after we'd gotten back here, but nothing came to me. Another low moan from behind me startled me as he pulled me into him even harder. This time, I could feel his rigid cock against my ass.

I lifted the edge of the blankets, trying hard not to wake him. I was relieved to see I was still completely clothed, even if it was only a pair of skimpy shorts and a tank top. I rested my head down on the fluffy pillow and tried to calm my breathing.

"Morning," he murmured, his gruff, sexy voice hitting me directly in my center as his hands gripped my waist.

"Ah, morning," I said, swallowing hard as the wave of

arousal passed through me at the feel of his hands on me, his hard cock pressing into my ass.

"Why are you awake so early?" he questioned, rolling onto his back to give me a little space. "I figured you'd sleep until noon with all the wine you drank last night."

"Spa day, remember," I said, kicking the covers off me and swinging my legs around to greet the coolness of the room. My head spun as I reached for my sweater that lay on the end of the bed. I quickly threw it over me, zipping up the front of it to hide my hardened nipples before turning to face him.

He chuckled. "You can relax. Nothing happened," he said knowingly, placing his arms behind his head.

I hated to admit it, but he looked devilishly sexy laying like that, and the longer I looked at him, the more I wished that something had happened between us.

"I know that," I said, trying hard to play it off; however, the quiver in my voice gave me away. I had absolutely no idea what had gone on last night.

"No, you were panicking, so I let you panic a little." He shrugged, placing his one hand down on his rock-hard abs. "You know you are really quite adorable in that state." He chuckled. "But you need to relax a little. It's not good for your body to hold on to all that tension."

I frowned. How dare he tell me I am adorable when I panic. I was just about to reply when he smiled.

"Relax, Tess, you were cold last night, and you insisted

that I come and warm you up. You were out in minutes, and I didn't have the heart to move you off my chest, you were so sound, so I stayed and watched TV. I must have fallen asleep." He sat up and ran both hands through his thick, dark hair.

I didn't know what to say, so instead, I just gave him a small smile.

"What do you want for breakfast?" he questioned.

I couldn't help but check him out as he kicked the covers off him and stood up. I watched his muscles ripple as he stood there and stretched, my eyes wandering down to his ass, which was framed perfectly in his boxer briefs.

"Earth to, Tess..." he called.

I blinked and brought my eyes to his face. "Bacon and abs." The instant the words fell from my lips, I realized what it was I had said, and I immediately wanted to curl up and die. "I mean eggs. Bacon and eggs."

He chuckled. "All right, let me order it while you shower." He shook his head, and as I turned and walked into the bathroom, I heard him laugh to himself and repeat what I had said. I wanted to die.

"We hope you enjoyed your day with us," the girl behind the counter said as I grabbed the small bag of products I had purchased from the spa.

"Oh, I did. Thank you." I checked inside the small bag to make sure I had everything. Then I walked over and slid my shoes on and deposited the slippers that they had given me to use into the basket marked 'used.'

I stepped out of the spa and made my way through the lobby of the hotel and over to the elevators. It had been an amazing day. It would have been more amazing had I been able to get Maddox out of my mind. Instead, he had stayed at the forefront of my mind the entire day, and during my massage, my mind kept drifting and I was sure it was his hands I felt running over my body.

I climbed into the elevator and leaned against the wall, trying hard to clear thoughts of him from my mind. I was to get changed and meet Maddox outside the hotel at six. We were going to take a walk down to the Eiffel Tower, and then we were going out for dinner.

I stood inside the room, pulling outfits out of my suitcase, trying hard to decide what on earth to wear. I had only brought a couple of dresses, and I wanted to save the black one for New Year's Eve. After numerous minutes of internal debate, I finally settled on a pair of black dress pants and a beige sweater. I checked the time, it was almost five thirty. I showered, got dressed, and then swept my hair up into a ponytail and looked at myself in the mirror.

Twenty minutes later, I looked at myself in the full-length mirror that hung inside the closet door completely unhappy with my outfit decision, I knew I should have packed a little better. "Guess it will have to do," I muttered, turning side to side to check myself in the mirror. I hadn't cared what I looked like as much as I suddenly did in a very long time.

"You look gorgeous."

I jumped at the deep voice behind me and turned around to see Maddox standing there in slightly baggy jeans, a sweater, and a three-quarter-length coat, a black scarf hung loosely around his neck. I followed his eyes as they ran the length of my body and back up to my face.

"I didn't even hear the door open."

"I was getting worried. You're normally twenty minutes early. You're almost ten minutes late."

I glanced down at my watch and then over to the clock beside the bed. "Ohhhh…" I said, tapping the face of my watch. "My watch must have stopped," I said, taking it off and laying it on the table.

"As long as you are okay. Are you ready?" he asked, holding his hand out.

Snow fell gently around us as we stood looking up at the amazement of the Eiffel Tower. "It's beautiful, isn't it?" I whispered.

"Sure is," Maddox whispered back.

When I glanced over to him, he wasn't even looking at the tower. His eyes were focused on me. I felt my cheeks heat and then looked back at the tower. "Oh, look at the lights," I said in amazement as the twinkling lights started up again. Again, when I turned to look at Maddox, he was still intently watching me, a calm, peaceful look on his face as he studied me.

"I really hate to do this, but we need to get going. We can come back later on, but we have reservations in five minutes," Maddox said, pulling me in the tower's direction.

I took a couple of steps forward and stopped. "The restaurant is this way," I insisted, trying to pull him back, but he stood his ground.

He looked at me and shook his head. "I changed it. We are now eating here. We have reservations on the second floor for seven."

I blinked and looked up at the tower, then looked to Maddox. I could feel the tears beginning to burn. I had written the idea down in my honeymoon planning journal and had only ever told Derrick about it, but he had quickly squashed the idea. "How did you know?" I questioned.

"I remember the fight, Tess," Maddox said, stepping closer, taking my hands in his. "I went to go into the kitchen and heard the things he had said to you. I heard you try to fight back, then I heard you cry. I heard it all."

I remembered the fight as well. I had brought it up at one of our wedding planning sessions with the wedding party. When I had gotten up to grab more drinks, Derrick had come into the kitchen behind me. I had thought he'd come in to help me carry out more drinks, but instead he closed the door behind him and, in a matter of moments, had basically made me wish this trip wasn't going to happen.

I'd thought no one had heard us fight, but I'd been wrong, and when we walked out of that kitchen, I put on my brave face and never brought it up to anyone ever again.

I looked up at the Eiffel Tower, the twinkling lights now blurring because of tears. Then I looked down at the ground, not wanting him to see my tears.

I felt his hand on my chin and the pressure as he gently raised my head and wiped the tears from my cheek with his thumb as he looked into my eyes. "Remember what I said. He deserves none of those tears."

His words made me cry even more. "You didn't have to do this," I said between tears.

"I know, but I did it, so let's not waste the reservation, okay. Besides, you deserve it. I mean, when do you think you are going to be back in Paris?" he asked, bringing his hand up to wipe away another tear from my cheek.

I glanced up at him, staring into his eyes. "Thank you," I said, leaning in and kissing him on the cheek.

"Don't thank me. Just please, do me one favour and just explain to me sometime over this trip what it was you ever saw in him, because I'm having a hard time figuring it out what a girl like you was doing with a guy like him," he whispered, his voice barely audible.

"I think I can do that," I whispered, looking up at the twinkling lights once again.

I looked at Maddox, a soft smile falling over my lips. Our eyes locked, and we stood there before the Eiffel Tower, and before I knew what was happening, he leaned in and placed a single kiss on my lips.

A surge of heat ran through my body the instant his lips touched mine, and I closed my eyes. We stayed that way for a few moments before he pulled away. "Shall we go?" he questioned, looking into my eyes.

I bit my bottom lip and nodded, and even though all I wanted was to feel his lips on mine again, I threaded my arm through his and allowed him to lead me toward the Eiffel Tower.

Dinner had been absolutely amazing, each course better than the previous. Once again, the conversation flowed between us, and it seemed all the tension that had been between us before was quelled with that kiss. As the night passed, I wished that we could have spent the entire night at the table, drinking and talking as we looked over the beauty of the city.

We now walked through the quiet streets of Paris, snow falling heavily. Maddox was quiet, and I clung to him so I didn't slip.

"Did you enjoy dinner?" he asked. It was the first thing either of us had said in over twenty minutes.

"Loved it. That meal—oh God, and those desserts... What amazing choices you picked." I smiled. We'd each ordered a main, and then each a different dessert. We both ate half, then switched, but the chocolate souffle had stuck out in my mind and how it practically melted in my mouth.

"Good, I am glad."

"You need to tell me what I owe you though."

Maddox abruptly stopped. "No way! That was my treat. My surprise."

I frowned. "No, you got dinner the other night. There is no way I am letting you pay for another meal when you are a guest on this trip."

Maddox stopped walking and turned to me. "I'm not telling you what that meal cost, Tess. But if you want to owe me then for payment, I want you to tell me what on earth you ever saw in Derrick. I figured you would have told me over dinner."

"I would have, but it would have ruined my appetite, and if you don't want to see my dinner in reverse, we don't need to talk about it now. Besides, your rule. We aren't supposed to mention his name, remember."

He stopped, taking both of my hands in his. "All right, you're right, but, please, let me treat you to whatever I want on this vacation, without a word of disagreement."

I had a hard time accepting that he wanted to do these things for me. When Derrick had done things like this, he was always looking for something in return.

"I wanted to treat you," he said, studying my eye. "I can imagine you're not used to that, but get used to it, at least for this trip."

"Okay," I said, biting my bottom lip and looking into his eyes.

As his eyes washed over my face, he didn't hesitate. He leaned in and slowly took my mouth with his, his tongue forcing my lips apart. I could feel the urgency in his kiss as his lips pressed firmly against mine, my body lighting up like a Christmas tree. When we parted, both of us breathless, no words were said. He took hold of my hand, and we continued our walk along the Seine River back to our hotel as if nothing happened.

Maddox

We enjoyed a few glasses of wine down in the lobby bar once we had returned from dinner. We sat in one of the booths, talking and drinking, while we watched the gentle falling snow turn into a blowing and quickly accumulating snowstorm. We sat watching in amazement as everything was bathed in white, while the other guests began panicking. This wasn't normal weather for Paris, and as the storm raged on, the bartender soon announced that they were closing the bar early so the hotel staff could make their way home safely.

We'd just gotten into our room, changed, and both of us settled for the night. Tess lay in bed, and I was back in my usual spot on the couch. We were right in the middle of a movie when the power flickered once then twice. The third time the room was bathed in darkness.

"Dammit, that was a good movie too. Now I'm never going to know how it ends," Tess cried.

I couldn't help but laugh out loud. "It wasn't that good, Tess."

"Oh stop, it was great." She giggled.

"Listen to that wind," I said as the wind howled outside.

"Yeah, it's pretty bad out there."

We lay there for half an hour listening to the howling winds, when I noticed how cool the room was beginning to get. The hotel was old, and it felt as if there wasn't much more than a piece of cardboard separating us from the weather outside.

"Going to be a cold one tonight," I said, getting up and making my way across the dark room to the desk. "I think the heat stopped working," I said, holding my hand near the old radiator on the wall. Sure enough, it was cool to the touch.

"What are you doing?"

"Calling the front desk for more blankets. We are going to need them, especially if the heat doesn't come back on. It hasn't been off all that long, and it's already getting cold in here." I picked up my cell phone and used the light from the screen to see the phone to dial the front desk. The phone rang and rang, but no one answered.

"Can't get through?" Tess questioned, and I could hear the quiver in her voice.

"No, they must be busy. There is no answer," I replied, hanging the phone up and walking to the closet to check and see if there were more blankets on another shelf that we may have missed, but it was empty.

"Just come lay with me for now, that way we will stay warm until we can get through to ask for some."

"Are you sure?"

Tess said nothing, but I could see the outline of her body sitting up in bed from what little light was coming through the window. I saw she flipped the covers back as she waited for me.

I slid into the bed beside her and pulled her into me, then pulled the blankets up around us. We were both lying there together in silence, listening to the wind howl. Holding her in my arms was definitely a feeling I could get used to if I allowed myself to, I thought, my cock hardening at that idea. I reached down and adjusted myself, trying to will my cock to go down, but the more she snuggled into me, the harder I got. Soon the idea of calling for more blankets escaped my mind, and the howling winds lulled us both into a deep sleep.

I woke suddenly and glanced around the dark room looking for the clock; the power was still out. It was cold even under the blankets, and I could still hear the wind whipping around outside the window.

I quickly slipped out of bed and I shivered as the cold air hit my warm skin. I grabbed the blanket that I had been using from the couch and threw it over top of Tess. Then I walked to the window and glanced outside. Snow covered everything in a thick blanket of white, and it was still snowing hard. As I stood there, I could feel the cold radiating off the glass, so I pulled the thick curtains closed over the window, hoping that would help to stop the room from getting any colder. Then I crawled back into the warm bed.

I had just gotten comfortable and was about to spoon up behind Tess when she shifted and rolled over, snuggling into my side. "So cold." She quivered.

"Lift your head," I whispered.

The second she did, I slid my arm under her neck and then rolled onto my side, wrapping my other arm around her, enveloping her in my warmth. She was cold to the touch, and she shivered against me. I closed my eyes. She felt so tiny in my arms and holding her this way felt so natural to me. It wasn't sexual, or perhaps it was, but I certainly wasn't ready to admit that to myself.

I let out a deep sigh, pulling her closer, and all I could think about was what kind of bro code I had broken by placing that kiss on her lips earlier tonight.

She adjusted herself in my arms, resting her head against my chest, and that was when I felt her arm wrap around my waist, while she snuggled even closer than I thought possible.

My cock jumped, hardening at the fact her body was

pressed so close against mine. I silently prayed that she couldn't feel me, but that thought went out of the window when I felt her place a tiny kiss on my chest, her hand travelling to my hip. My heart was beating so hard I was sure she could feel it through my chest, and my dick was pulsing as I concentrated on her hand.

I knew she felt me, and that thought turned me on more than anything. I wanted her to touch me so badly but had to chase that thought away or else I was going to act on how I was feeling. Then I felt her lips deliver another tiny kiss against my chest. I let out a small groan, gripping her hip, as she, too, let out a tiny moan. I didn't wait. I couldn't. I rolled myself up onto my elbow and brought my free hand to her cheek and brought my lips to hers.

I felt her small hand grip my hip as my tongue parted her lips, washing through her mouth, and when I sucked on her bottom lip, she let out sexiest little moan, which was almost my undoing. My cock was so hard that it hurt, and I prayed that she'd put her hand on me, anything to stop the constant ache.

I squeezed her hip, pulling her as close to me as I could, kissing her hard, making sure she felt me. I wanted her to know how attracted I was to her, and I ground against her again. Our lips parted, and I lay back down, breathless, as my mind spun. I closed my eyes and that was when I felt her hand run over the front of my boxers. I went to take her hand when she surprised me by straddling my waist and raising her body on top of mine. I could feel the heat from between her legs and could only imagine how wet she must have been.

I wrapped my arms around her body as she kissed me with as much passion as I had kissed her, only this time I felt her hips rotate as she ground down onto me. I gripped her hips with my hands, praying that she would stop. It had been so long since I had been with a woman, and knew I wouldn't be able to take much without embarrassing myself, but it didn't stop her.

I watched in the shadows of the darkness as she sat up and pulled her shirt off over her head, her hardened nipples calling to me. "Touch me, Maddox. Please," she murmured, bringing her lips to mine.

I swallowed hard as I allowed my hands to travel up to her full breasts. Cupping them in my hands, I ran my thumbs over her already hardened nipples. I sat up and took one into my mouth as I pulled the covers up around her to keep her warm. The instant I had sucked her into my mouth, she dropped her head back and let out this deep moan that went straight to my cock. I then took the other into my mouth, repeating exactly what I had done. She rocked her hips against me as I pulled her into my arms.

"God you're beautiful," I whispered as I brushed a strand of hair out of her eyes. I could tell even in the darkness that her eyes were full of want and need. I pulled her down on top of me, rolled her over, and took her mouth with mine.

I didn't want to admit it to myself, but over the past few days, I had begun to feel for this woman who lay in my arms. I hadn't wanted to admit it to myself that there was something between us, but through each small touch and each slight gesture, the fog had finally cleared.

Now, as I held her, almost naked beneath me, my hands gripping her waist as I kissed her, I knew deep in my soul that I was in trouble. I just prayed that we took our time and that we didn't rush things. I didn't want to scare her away from me.

Tess

When I woke the next morning, the power had been restored, and the room was back to its normal temperature. I'd slipped out of bed and into the shower. I stood underneath the warm spray and closed my eyes. The memories of last night flashing before my eyes. I could feel his urgent kiss, his hands as they roamed parts of my body, the way his mouth felt as he sucked my hardened nipples into his mouth. I could hear his ragged breathing as I ground myself down onto him, his soft moans as I repeated those moves over and over, until he finally flipped me over onto my back. As I stood there, I could feel my centre begin to throb as those memories ran through my mind, and I leaned up against the wall and placed my fingers between my legs.

I had dressed and had just hung up the phone from

ordering breakfast when Maddox woke. I could feel the tension rising in the room and I swallowed hard as he climbed out of bed. I watched as he stretched, I had no idea how to react to what had happened between us. I didn't know how he was going to react to what had happened. I dug deep trying to find the words I wanted to say as he walked over to me. He placed his hand on my shoulder, bent down and placed a single kiss on my lips.

"Morning." His eyes met mine, and then he met my lips one more time, pulling me against him, before he made his way into the bathroom.

There was nothing else said about what had happened the night before between us, and if it hadn't been for that morning kiss, I would have thought he hadn't remembered what had happened.

We spent our last day in Paris touring some museums. We walked together, sharing small, intimate glances as we held hands. We focused our attention on one another, instead of on the artifacts of each museum. We talked silently through touches and glances, looking into one another's eyes, saying more to one another than could have been possible with words.

It was still hard for me to believe what had happened between us in the early-morning hours, my mind constantly going back to that first deep kiss. His kiss was like no other I had experienced before, and if I were being open and honest with myself, I couldn't wait for the next one.

It was a new feeling for me to be so perfectly in sync with someone that I almost didn't know how to handle it. I'd never been like this with Derrick or any of the other guys I'd been with. But I needed to stop myself because Maddox and I weren't together. Then a question popped into my head: what were we to one another? Instead of allowing my thoughts to overtake, I cleared my mind, slipped my hand into his, and tried not to overthink things.

When we returned from the museum, we took our time packing our things, preparing for the move to Le Mont-Dore in the morning. It was a full day of travel, and even though I knew Maddox was looking forward to spending some time on the slopes, neither of us were really looking forward to losing an entire day travelling.

"What do you say we order in some room service? Perhaps, add in a bottle of that wine we both love?" he asked while picking up his bag and placing it by the door. I stood at the edge of the bed, struggling with the lock on my bag as he waited for my response. "Here, let me," he said, coming over, wrapping his arms around me from behind. My entire body was on fire as I felt the heat from his body and his scent surround me. His hands covered mine as he slipped the lock from my fingers and fiddled with it.

When the lock finally clicked shut, I looked up at him. "Thank you," I whispered as our eyes locked, and we stood there for a moment, until he finally brought his lips to mine for a quick kiss, which turned deeper. I closed my eyes as his lips danced over mine and felt a large void when he pulled away.

"That sounds...fantastic," I said, looking up at him.

"It does sound fantastic," he said breathlessly as he bent his head and brought his lips to mine once again, his hand resting on my lower abdomen, pulling me back against him as he kissed me deeper this time.

I could already feel his arousal through his jeans and wanted more, but he pulled away. My body screamed. I didn't want him to stop, yet I was afraid to do anything that would bring him back.

He picked up my bag and placed it down beside his. "All right then, let's take a peek at the menu and decide what we want," he said, throwing the room service menu down on the edge of the bed, moving to lean against the desk.

I could feel him watch me as I read over the menu. I'd finally made a choice, and while he called for the food, I checked to make sure I had our tickets ready for the train tomorrow.

We shared food, some wine, and watched a movie, and then, as if it were a normal occurrence between us, we fell into bed together for the first time without reason. Only tonight, there was no kissing nor messing around. He simply pulled me into his arms and held me until the warmth of his body enveloped me and we fell asleep.

I woke in the middle of the night, panic filling me. I sat up and looked around the room and then to Maddox, who slept soundly beside me, trying to catch my breath.

I slipped from the bed, getting up to grab a drink of water. I filled the glass and stood in the bathroom drinking down the cool liquid, looking at my reflection in the mirror. My mind was running over all that had happened over the past few weeks.

First, Derrick popped into my mind, reliving our relationship and how distant we truly had been. The relationship had been so toxic and blinding, or perhaps it was my thoughts of what I wanted our relationship to be and that was what had blinded me, turning everything toxic. I'd been so caught up in the security he offered, I saw nothing else. I wanted to believe that I had been the right one for him, but now, as I stood looking at myself, I wondered if I was ever going to be right for anyone.

I could feel a deep lump forming in my throat, making it hard for me to breathe as I fought back the tears that were threatening to fall. I re-filled the glass with water and sipped it slowly until that lump disappeared.

Then I looked at myself, at the way I had dealt with Derrick telling me he had cheated. Had it hurt? Yes. Had it been my fault? No. He had done these things under his own volition, no one else's. I thought back to all the times he had yelled or disapproved of something I had done, when in fact he should have supported me. I thought back to all the times he had left me at home or hadn't come home, and I wondered if those had been the nights he'd been with other woman, but deep down I knew the answer. Maddox was right, he didn't deserve my tears; he didn't deserve another thought.

I walked back into the bedroom and glanced at the bed where Maddox slept, his back toward me. Then I glanced over to the couch, wondering if I shouldn't just take the blanket and curl up over there instead of sleeping beside him, but then I looked back to the bed and thought back to the warmth he offered. I let out a breath and, without giving it another thought, climbed back into bed and curled up under the covers. I'd just gotten comfortable when Maddox rolled over to face me. I took this moment to watch him as he slept, to study the softness in his face.

As I watched him, his story came to the front of my mind. I remembered his face as he told me about Jenn, and I felt my heart break as I tried to even comprehend the pain he must have felt at such a young age. Most people, after experiencing something like that, would have changed and become cold and afraid to love. Yet none of that seemed true about Maddox.

He was different, and even though we weren't in a relationship, I could totally see myself getting hooked on him. Even though I hadn't suffered the same loss he had, there was a part of me that was petrified of letting him in. I wondered if he too felt this way, afraid to let someone in again. I was afraid of having a repeat of what had just happened. What if I got involved with Maddox only to find out that I wasn't enough for him either? That he wanted more than I could give. The fear of that happening was completely ingrained in me. Then his words ran through my head about how a real man would have stood before me and told me the truth before he bedded another. Those words did offer me some kind of comfort, giving me a glimpse into the type of man he really was.

I rolled over and faced the room. I had to break this thought cycle if I were going to get any more sleep. I closed my eyes and did my best to relax. I steadied my breathing and was just about asleep when I felt Maddox wrap an arm around my waist and pull me against him. He placed a gentle kiss on the crook of my neck, and soon he was breathing lightly against me.

As I lay there wrapped in his arms, I knew there was

no way I should compare either of these men to one another because each of them were so different that I already knew there was absolutely no comparison.

Then, without warning, a thought ran through my head that shocked me. What if Derrick had been the wrong choice for me from the beginning? That the only way I ever would have met this man lying beside me was for me to go through all of this. Perhaps this experience had taught me I needed a man, one who wasn't afraid to show his love, one who supported me no matter what, not one who only did so at his convenience. I needed to be made to feel special. I needed someone to lean on when things went wrong, and I needed someone who loved me for who I was, not for who they wanted me to be, and in return I would give all those things back. It was then, in the moments of the wee hours of the morning, as I lay in his arms, that the realization came to me, that it was time to take what I deserved and to be okay with it.

I closed my eyes as a sense of peace came over me as those thoughts had run through my head. I felt the slight puff of breath against my skin, and then Maddox kissed me once again, pulling me tighter into him. A surge of excitement ran through my body. I closed my eyes tight and allowed that feeling to flow right through me. I realized in that moment it was too late to stop how I was feeling. Who was I trying to kid? I was already hooked on him, and I just prayed that he, too, was hooked on me, and I'd never have to worry about him breaking my heart.

It was a little after nine when we finally arrived at the door to our private chalet. We were both exhausted from the long day of travel, and we waited patiently as the bellhop brought our luggage from the small golf cart-like vehicle up to the door.

"We hope you enjoy your stay with us," he said, inserting the key and turning the lock. He pushed the door open and turned on the lights. We stepped into a sunken living room with an enormous stone fireplace, a fire already lit. We had a perfect view of the ski hills, lined with white lights as little black bodies scurried down the hills. I watched as Maddox walked over to the window and glanced out, then turned and looked at me, smiling.

"Amazing view," he said, looking back out the window.

"Yes, one of our very best," the bellhop said as he placed our bags on the floor just inside the door. "There is a small kitchen to your left, bathroom with large jacuzzi tub right over there," he said, pointing to a door, "and in here is your bedroom, complete with fireplace and California-king bed."

I couldn't help but take a peek into the bedroom. I could see the ski hills from there as well, and the fireplace in the bedroom was lit as well, casting a soft glow over the room. "It's beautiful," I said, smiling, coming back into the sunken living room and running my hand along the back of the couch.

"Sir, I see you have ski time booked tomorrow morning at nine. It's quite a distance. Will you be needing a shuttle down?"

Maddox turned and looked at me and I nodded. "Yes, he will." There was no way I was letting him out of skiing. He had been so good to me over this trip. "Is it possible for you to arrange that for him?" I questioned, waiting for the bellhop to answer.

"Yes, absolutely, miss."

Maddox cleared his throat. "Actually, is it possible for you to move my ski time to say eleven?" he asked, looking over at me.

"Certainly, sir. I will be here to pick you up a half hour before. What time shall I send breakfast?"

Maddox looked to me and I to him, then he shrugged. "Nine-thirty?"

I nodded, staring back at him, as if we were the only two in the room.

"That sounds fine, sir. I'll just leave the keys to your room here," he said, setting them down on the table that sat inside the door. "Have a good night."

We both stood staring at one another, neither of us saying anything, as the bellhop walked to the door and let himself out.

The second the door was closed, Maddox walked over to me and took both of my hands in his. "You know, I don't need to ski tomorrow. It is New Year's Eve, after all. We can always do something else."

"Oh, but you do. I have a spa day planned, a mud bath followed by a massage with essential oils, and then we will party the night away." I smiled, meeting his eyes. "Now I should go unpack our things."

I went to walk away, but Maddox stopped me, putting his arms up on either side of my head and leaning against the wall I was standing in front of, blocking me in. I could see a playful glint in his eyes and could feel my body begin to respond to the sexual tension between us.

"Maddox, it's been a long day…please. I'm exhausted. I just really want to get this done so I can relax," I said, clasping my fingers with his.

"We can't have that," he whispered and brought his lips to mine, wrapping me in his arms.

"Can't have what?" I asked.

"Have you getting irritated? I can hear it in your voice," he whispered.

I could feel his breath on my cheek and a surge of electricity ran through my body.

As his tongue parted my lips and washed through my

mouth, I closed my eyes. His kiss made me forget everything that I had been planning to do. I brought my arms up around his neck and relaxed against the wall. He sucked my bottom lip into his mouth, then swept his tongue through my mouth again. He lifted me off the ground and carried me into the bedroom, kicking the door shut behind him.

Maddox

New Year's Eve

I stood in the lobby of the main lodge with a drink in my hand, while people from all over the resort were heading into the event hall for the New Year's Eve celebration the ski resort was putting on. I'd finished skiing earlier than expected and made my way back to the room to get ready while Tess was still at the spa.

"Another drink, sir?" a young woman asked, holding out a tray of drinks.

"Thanks." I switched my empty glass for a full one and then glanced down at my watch. It was almost seven. Dinner was going to be starting soon. I did not know why she wasn't here yet, and I ran my hand through my hair in frustration as I tried to calm my nerves, when I turned around to see Tess slip into the building.

My eyes instinctively ran the length of her body. She looked stunning in the black dress she wore, and my eyes danced over her curves. She looked around the room, searching the crowd, her eyes brightening the second they landed on me.

"Hey, sorry, I had trouble with the zipper on this dress," she said, her cheeks turning a shade of pink as she took a glass of champagne from a server.

"You should have called me. I could have helped you with that zipper." I winked, placing my hand on her lower back.

She crinkled her nose. "Not sure that was the type of help I needed, but thank you." She giggled, taking a sip of her drink, meeting my eyes.

"You have no idea what kind of help I was going to offer. I just happen to be an expert at zippers." I chuckled and leaned down and kissed her cheek.

"I'm sure you are," she said, rolling her eyes at me and laughing.

"We should probably get in and get a table."

"You are probably right. Besides, I am starving."

"Can't have you starving. You need your strength." I winked. "Come, let's go." I placed my hand on her lower back and guided her into the event hall.

It took a bit, but we finally found an unoccupied table

for two and took our seat just in time to for the food to be served.

I placed my spoon down on the table and looked over at Tess, who had just put the last spoonful of dessert in her mouth. "Looks like you are really enjoying that."

"So good," she said, leaning back against her seat as the music played.

"Would you like another drink?" I asked.

"I would love one."

"All right, you stay here. I'll be right back."

I looked over my shoulder at her sitting at the table as I made my way through the crowd. I didn't want to take my eyes off her. Music was playing and people were dancing as the music played. I carried our drinks back to the table we'd been sitting at only to find it empty.

I looked out onto the dance floor, trying to find Tess, but couldn't see her anywhere. When I turned back around, I spotted her. She was standing outside on the balcony off the hall.

She stood there, holding her phone in her hands as she typed feverishly away, a frown on her face. I watched as the screen lit up on her phone and she stomped her foot, quickly typing again. *What the hell was going on?*

Again, the screen lit up, only this time she didn't bother to respond. Instead she shoved her phone into her purse and wrapped my suit jacket over her bare shoulders, staring out to the ski hills.

I watched her for a moment through the window, leaning against the concrete ledge. Whatever that had been about it had seemed to take her a million miles away. I watched as she stood looking out over the ski hills, and I frowned when I saw her bring her hand up and wipe her cheek. I left our drinks on the table and made my way over to the closest door that led outside.

She turned in time to see me step outside. "Hey," she whispered, a soft smile coming to her lips.

"Hey. What are you doing out here?" I questioned, going over to her, wrapping my arms around her to warm her. I hoped she would talk to me without me having to pry. I wanted her to trust me, to talk to me, to confide in me.

"Just thinking."

"Uh oh, that is never good after copious amounts of alcohol. What about?"

"Tell me about it." Tess laughed, and then shrugged, her face turning serious as she looked across the way at the lit ski hills. "One should never think too hard about anything," she whispered, leaning back against me, going quiet again.

I wrapped my arms around her and held her tight, resting my chin on her head, and instantly I wondered if it was probably Derrick who had messaged her.

"Well, if you aren't going to tell me what's going

through your mind, I say we head inside and dance for a bit."

Tess stood there in my arms, leaning against me, and then whispered, "Just a few more minutes. I'd just like to stand here wrapped in your arms for a few more minutes."

I frowned and held her tighter, wondering what the hell had made her say that to me. I held her until she took my hand in hers and pulled me inside.

The party was in full swing. People were dancing, drinks were pouring, and appetizers were being served. We danced and drank for hours, and the longer I held her in my arms, the more comfortable I felt. The party was wild, and before we knew it, the time to countdown to the new year was almost here.

They brought around glasses of champagne for everyone, and we stood surrounded by couples as we began the countdown to the new year.

"Ten... Nine... Eight..."

I turned Tess around so she was facing me and looked down into her eyes.

"Seven... Six... Five..." We counted together. She looked up at me and smiled, resting her hand on my chest.

"Four... Three... Two..." I nibbled at her lips as we continued to count down together.

"... One. Happy New Year!" We both yelled at the same time. Music blared and confetti fell from the ceiling. I pulled her tightly against me, leaned down, and met her lips as she wrapped her arms around my neck, kissing me back.

Our lips danced over one another's as the surrounding crowd cheered, some couples kissing, some blowing into their noisemakers, and others swaying to the music. To me, even though all that chaos surrounded us, it felt as if we were the only two in the room. The longer we kissed and the closer I pulled her to me, the more excited I got, and all I wanted to do was take her back to the room and have my way with her.

"Happy New Year," she whispered as my lips travelled down her neck. She let out a soft moan as she ran her fingers through my hair, and when I pulled away, the look in her eyes begged me to bring my lips back to hers, which I happily obliged.

We returned to the room to find a card on the door. I opened the note and read it aloud. "Your turndown service has been completed."

Tess let out a giggle. "God, what else did I forgot to cancel," she said, laughing as she stepped inside of the room in front of me.

My eyes were trained on her ass as she walked into the chalet, looking around for whatever surprise awaited us.

"What did you forget?" I questioned, kicking my shoes off.

"Um...a hot bath, chocolate-covered strawberries, and champagne," she said, hiding her face in her hands as she stood outside the bathroom door laughing.

I walked over and placed my hands on her waist, kissing her neck as I ran my hands down her hips. "That doesn't sound so bad."

"It doesn't?" she questioned, as she dipped her head to the side to give me better access.

I shook my head, then in one swift motion, I lifted her into the air and threw her over my shoulder.

"Maddox." She laughed. "Put me down."

"No." I laughed, tapping her ass with my hand as I carried her into the enormous bathroom. I placed her down on the tile floor, brought my hands to her cheeks, and kissed her deeply.

Her eyes were full of want as I unbuttoned my shirt, her eyes falling to my bare chest. I pulled the tail of my shirt from my pants and pulled it from my shoulders, allowing it to fall on the floor.

Her cheeks flushed, she reached out and shyly took hold of my belt, slowly opening it. Her fingers flicked at the button on my pants, and she worked the zipper, then slid those down over my hips. My cock was already hard, her eyes dancing over the rigid outline in my boxers, but she didn't touch me. Instead, she turned around, placed both of her hands on the counter, and looked at me in the mirror. Her eyes were full of want, practically begging for me to take her right there on the spot.

I kissed the back of her neck and pulled at the zipper on the back of her dress, the sound echoing through the bathroom as I lowered it. "Told you I was an expert at zippers," I whispered as I pushed the dress off her shoulders and slipped the material down her body.

As her dress piled at her feet, I looked at her in the mirror, my eyes running over her bra and panty-clad body, and then brought my hands up to the hook on her bra, and without my fingers touching her skin I unhooked it, the material falling away from her full breasts.

She turned around and looked up at me with innocent eyes, and I bent down and met her lips, quickly forgetting about the strawberries, the champagne, and the full bath behind us. Instead, I picked her up and carried her out of the bathroom, across the living room, and into the bedroom.

Tess

I could feel his arousal on my belly as he carried me into the bedroom.

"I want you," he murmured between kisses. "Every fucking inch of you," he whispered, running his hand through my hair as he kissed me hard.

I wanted him, too, but I was terrified to say the words out loud. I gripped his shoulders as I let myself get lost in him.

I fell onto the plush mattress and looked up at him as he stood over me, his eyes roaming my body. Every inch of my body was on fire, and every touch he bestowed upon me was electrified. He looked down at me, his eyes consuming my body as they ran over me.

He reached out and brushed his fingers along my panties. Bending down, he kissed my belly just above my panty line, and I arched my back off the mattress and let out a loud moan.

The second his lips left my body, I opened my eyes and looked up at him. He stood before me. I followed his hands as he gripped his hard cock through his boxers, then pushed them down, allowing them to fall to the floor at his feet.

My eyes washed over his chest, his rock-hard abs, and then down to his manhood. I bit my bottom lip and looked up at him and met his eyes. Everything about him was perfect. He brought his hands to my waist, pulling at my panties. I lifted myself up and closed my eyes as he slowly removed them, his fingers skimming down my legs. I fought back the moan as he leaned down onto the bed and brought his lips to mine.

"God, you are fucking perfect," he whispered, his hands roaming my body as he kissed me.

My skin pebbled at his touch, his lips dancing down my body. A soft moan escaped my lips as he licked and sucked at my breasts, while his fingers moved between my legs, finally sliding them through my hot, wet center. My hands gripped his bicep as he slid one and then two fingers inside me, while his thumb rubbed my clit in small circles.

He met my lips as I took him in my hand, a low, throaty growl coming from him as I stroked him, my hand sliding gently over the smooth skin of his thick cock. He pulled his fingers from me, brought them to his mouth, and licked them both clean as he met my eyes.

"You taste fucking amazing," he murmured as he fell back onto the bed and closed his eyes, while I continued to stroke him.

"Fuck," he whispered as I ran my thumb over the head of his cock, smearing the bead of pre-cum over him. I kissed his chest and was about to make my way down to take him in my mouth when he stopped me. Instead, he rolled me over and kissed me hard, pulling my hand off him and holding it at the side of my head.

"It's been so long..." he murmured. "I'm probably not going to last too long." He ran his fingers through my hair, kissing me again.

"It's okay," I whispered, even though panic filled me. Was I the first girl he'd been with since Jenn? There was no way that could even be possible. Was it? I swallowed hard, trying to figure out if I should say anything at all, but he brought me right back into the moment by kissing me again.

He pulled his lips from mine and reached into the drawer of the nightstand, pulling out a condom. I took him in my hand again and just let myself feel the weight of him as I gently stroked him, watching as he ripped the package open and slid the condom over himself.

He removed my hand from him, took both of my hands and held them gently beside my head. Then he got onto his knees and positioned himself between my legs and pushed gently on the inside of my knees, spreading me open.

I watched as his eyes ran over my body. Excitement built in me as I watched him bend down and run his tongue through my slick center, concentrating on my clit. I arched my back off the mattress as his hands dug into my hips, holding me in place. He knelt down on the bed and placed each of my legs either side of his hips. He laced his fingers through mine, kissed me deeply, and took his cock in one hand and ran himself through my slick centre, placing himself at my opening and gently pushing himself deep inside.

He let out a hard breath as he held himself inside of me, allowing us both to adjust to the feel of one another. He kissed me as my body tightened around him. He pumped into me, shallow at first, then slow and deep, never once breaking our kiss or his rhythm.

I could feel my orgasm building only a couple of minutes after he was inside of me. Pulling my hands from his, I dug my fingers into his back while he gripped my waist, holding me still as he pumped deeply inside of me, his breathing growing rapid.

"God, you feel fucking amazing," he rasped, a sheen of sweat covering him.

Between his words and the feel of him, I could barely hold back, and I tightened around him, letting myself go, my moan filling the room. He pumped harder and faster the more I tightened around him, and within seconds, I could feel him pulse inside me as he emptied himself, his moan now filling the room. He leaned down, breathing hard, and met my lips, allowing his body to collapse on top of mine.

    I lay there with my eyes closed, trying hard to catch my breath. He pulled himself from me and disappeared into the bathroom. A few moments later, I felt the blankets move, and he slid into the bed. I rolled over to meet him, allowing him to pull me against him. He held me tightly in his arms, my head resting on his chest, as he kissed me gently.

Maddox

"Here, let me grab that," I said, getting up to remove the tray of empty dishes from her lap and stacking it on top of mine. I carried them out to the door and placed them outside, the cold hitting me as I set the tray on the ground outside. I quickly closed and locked the door, and then made my way back to the bedroom.

We had woken late, and with the snow falling hard outside, we had mutually agreed to spend our last day of vacation in bed together.

I closed the bedroom door quietly and dropped my robe. Tess lay on her back, her eyes closed. We'd had sex multiple times throughout the night, and just like me, she, too, was exhausted. I did my best not to disturb her and threw the blankets back so I could slide in under the covers.

She surprised me when I had gotten comfortable by sliding over to me wrapping her arms around me. I pulled her warm body against me and relaxed back into bed.

"Happy New Year," I whispered.

She looked up at me and pressed her lips to mine. "Happy New Year," she whispered, looking into my eyes.

She was so beautiful as she lay there, her hair mussed. I ran my fingers through her hair, placing my hand at the back of her head, and pulled her close for a kiss.

"Are you sure you don't want to do anything today?"

She looked at me with heady eyes and nodded, sucking her swollen lip into her mouth.

"We can do anything you want," I said, running my finger along that pouty lip.

"Anything?"

"Anything," I repeated. "All you need to do is say the word. We can shop, go snowshoeing, skiing if you're up for it, whatever you want, just say it."

I had expected her to reply with something in mind, but she surprised me by giggling at my suggestions and shook her head. "What I have in mind doesn't require us leaving this room,"

she replied shyly, sliding down under the covers. I inhaled deeply as she took my cock into her hot mouth.

"Fuck me..." I murmured under my breath as I enjoyed the feeling of her mouth on me.

I heard a tiny giggle, and once again her mouth was on

me, her tongue running around me. I closed my eyes and let myself relax as she continued, and then I pushed the blankets to the side and put my arm behind my head, adjusting the pillow so I could watch her as she took me deep into her mouth again.

"Is this what you want to do today?" I breathed hard as I watched my cock disappear into her mouth repeatedly, her eyes meeting mine with a playful glint. She held my cock in her hand and ran her tongue from the base to the tip before she nodded her yes.

I reached over to the nightstand drawer and reached inside, pulling another condom from the box. "All right, baby, get ready."

Her eyes widened, and she watched while I ripped the package open.

We had spent the entire day in bed wrapped in one another's arms, alternating between resting and sex. We had gotten up around five, ordered in some dinner, eaten, and then took some time to pack our bags. I now sat on the couch, trying to slow my thoughts, while I watched the news while Tess was in the shower.

What the hell was this that had happened? What were we to one another? Those were the only questions that kept running through my head as I sat there staring at the TV. I grabbed the remote, silencing the TV, and leaned back against the couch, resting my head back on the pillows as I stared at the screen. There was so much I had wanted to talk to Tess about today. I'd had an amazing trip, and the connection I felt between us was something I hadn't felt since Jenn.

I wanted to talk to her about how she felt and where she wanted things to go between us once we returned home, but I didn't know how to broach the subject. Part of me wasn't sure she was even ready to be entering another relationship so soon after Derrick.

I stood up and began pacing in front of the couch, my mind running in all directions as I tried to come up with what I should say to her. I could always tell her I wanted to see where we could go, or I could just tell her right upfront about how I felt and lay my heart right out on the line, risking the fact that her answer could in fact break mine into pieces. But I shook my head no, worrying that if I did that, she might think I was pressuring her into answering me. The last thing I wanted to do was scare her away.

I got up and paced back and forth across the living room, muttering to myself the words I thought I could say, when I heard a noise behind me.

I twisted around to see Tess standing just outside the bathroom door, wrapped in a towel, staring at me.

"What are you doing?" she questioned, a frown on her face.

"Nothing..." I quickly answered, swallowing hard.

"Doesn't look like nothing."

"What does it look like?"

"It looks like you're planning on telling me some sort of bad news."

I let out a laugh, only instead of stopping, I just continued laughing. If she thought for a second I was going to tell her bad news, she was crazy. The only bad news here was that I was crazy about her and had no idea how to tell her.

"Are you sure you're okay? You are acting totally weird," Tess said with her eyes glued to me as she walked by me, heading into the bedroom.

"I swear it's all good."

She gave me an unsure look and then took a couple steps into the room. "All right, as long as you're sure. I am heading to bed. Morning comes early."

I watched as she walked into the bedroom and began to relax, until she came back out. "Are you coming?"

She stood there gripping the towel in her hands, and in my mind, I wished she would drop it and entice me into the bedroom, making me forget everything that was running through my mind. I wanted to stay right in this moment forever. I nodded. "I'll be right in."

She simply nodded and walked into the bedroom. I sat

down on the couch and put my head in my hands, taking a moment to think about what I was about to do. I searched my thoughts, wondering if I was only feeling this way because she had been the first since Jenn. Although, the longer I searched my mind and my heart, I knew that what I was feeling was indeed very real. I'd always known it would be when I finally took that step.

My insides screamed at me to just tell her, but there was that tiny nagging voice in the back of my mind that instilled every doubt that every man felt at least once in their life. Instead of going with my heart, I allowed that tiny voice to take over and win, and to talk me out of exposing my heart.

I wasn't here to make her fall in love with me. I wasn't here to become her man. I was here because she didn't want to travel alone. This entire vacation would soon become a distant memory, just like Jenn had. We'd return home, time would pass, she would meet someone else, and I would watch her slip away from me.

"Baby, you coming to bed?" I heard her call from the bedroom in a sleepy voice.

"Yep, sorry," I called, standing up and shutting off all the lights, making my way into the bedroom.

I walked in to see her lying with her back toward me. I pulled the covers back and climbed into bed, but instead of wrapping my arm around her and pulling her into me, I rolled onto my side, facing away from her. I lay there for a few moments before I felt her hand on my shoulder.

"Is something wrong?" she questioned, her voice trembling.

"No, sweetie, nothing," I answered.

Silence hung between us until she cleared her throat. "It would be really nice if we spent our last night cuddling."

Our last night. There it was, I thought to myself as I closed my eyes tightly, not sure if I wanted to risk getting any closer to her than I already had. It had been a mistake to risk getting this close, but the second I looked over my shoulder into her eyes, there was no way I could deny her.

"Sorry, I figured you were almost asleep and didn't want to disturb you," I lied, rolling onto my back. The second I opened my arm to her, she slid into my side, placing her leg over mine, resting her head on my chest.

I wrapped my arm around her, bringing the other over to rest on her arm, and closed my eyes, kissing her gently on the forehead. It didn't take Tess long to drift off to sleep—it never did when she lay in my arms—but I laid awake all night, wrestling with my decision.

Tess

We'd been on the plane for over an hour. I looked out the window, deep within my own thoughts, as Maddox slept beside me. I rested my head back against the seat and zipped up my sweatshirt. I felt cold and pulled the small blanket the airline had provided around my shoulders. I had been trying to relax for the past hour, but it was proving to be useless. I felt heavier now than I had when I had boarded the plane to come here.

I'd had a bad feeling when I'd woken up this morning. I woke before the alarm, stretched, and went to roll over to cuddle into Maddox, but the bed was empty. When I'd placed my hand in his indent, the sheets were cold, that told me he'd been up for a while. I'd found him laying out on the couch in the living room watching TV, and I'd never have thought anything of it if he hadn't been so strange the night before.

I closed my eyes, thinking back over the past ten days and how much I had enjoyed my time. Not only my time in Paris, but my time with Maddox. As the memories danced through my mind, I realized just how at peace I had been during this time away. Derrick was now a distant memory, and Maddox was the only one who sat at the forefront of my mind.

I looked over at him and studied his strong features. I watched the rise and fall of his chest and looked down to his large, muscular hands as they rested clasped together against his stomach. I could still feel them on me. I could still feel his body against mine as he held me in his arms and, for a quick moment, wished that he was holding me now.

I watched him as he slept, the same question running through my mind that had been there for the past few days. What were we to one another? Were we friends? Friends with benefits? Or had we ruined our friendship by the line we had crossed with one another? Perhaps that was what he was going to tell me last night, that he was sorry, but after all we had been through, we were over. I swallowed hard at the thought as my eyes burned with tears. I really hoped that wasn't the case because I didn't want to lose my friendship with him over that.

I closed my eyes and swallowed hard. I didn't want to

return to reality if he would not be in my life. I wondered what life was going to look like now that I was returning home. I also feared all the questions I'd be asked. Laura would take one look at me and know what had happened between us. I blew out a breath, hoping that there would be some time before I got to see her because I wasn't ready to answer the barrage of questions I knew would be coming.

I watched him sleep, and it surprised me when a tear rolled down my cheek. That familiar lump that made it near impossible to swallow had returned. I reached up and wiped the tear away and tried to take in a deep breath, but my chest hurt so badly I couldn't. Everything I'd been feeling was coming to the surface, and I had no idea how to handle it.

"Tess?" I heard a deep voice ask. "What's wrong?"

I opened my eyes and realized that Maddox was awake and had been watching me as I sat there staring at him. A look of concern lined his face.

I shook my head, but no words came. Instead, the tears flowed freely, and I had absolutely no chance of stopping them. He said nothing. Instead he lifted the armrest that was between us, reclined our seats, and wrapped his arm around me, pulling me against him, where at the comfort of his touch the tears finally stopped.

I turned my key in the lock and pushed the door to my house open and stepped inside. I flipped the light on inside and slid out of my coat, hanging it on the hook just inside the door when Maddox appeared at the door with my bags.

He stepped into the house and placed them on the floor at the bottom of the stairs. "Did you want me to take them up for you?" he questioned.

"I'll be good. I need to do all the laundry anyway." I shrugged, looking over my shoulder in the direction of the laundry room. We both stood there looking awkwardly at one another as silence fell around us.

"Well, I guess I should get going," he said, glancing over his shoulder at his truck that was sat idling in the driveway.

Every part of me screamed not to let him go. Instead, I nodded. "It's been a long day," I whispered.

"It has," he agreed, his eyes meeting mine.

"Thank you for an absolutely amazing trip," he said, shoving his hands in his pockets, his body tensing as he stood there looking at me.

"No, thank you," I said, swallowing hard, trying to hide the tears that I could once again feel forming behind my eyes.

We stood in the entryway of my home staring at one another, the first awkward silence falling between us out of the entire trip.

"I guess that's it then."

My eyes washed over his large frame, wishing that I could once again be held in his arms. "I guess so." I shrugged.

"All right then, I guess I will see you around." He stood there, not moving, just watching me.

I swallowed hard and nodded. The air between us was growing thick with tension, making it almost impossible for me to breathe. Yet instead of saying anything to him, I allowed him to turn without another word and walk out the front door. When I heard the door click shut, I did everything I could to stop the tears from falling, but there was no stopping them. I thought about grabbing my bags and going about my business, but then I found myself walking into the living room and parting the blinds. I watched through the window as he climbed into his truck, but instead of reversing, he just sat there.

"Come back, Maddox. Please, come back," I whispered to myself. Perhaps if I willed him hard enough, or said it loud enough, it would happen. He would come walking back through my door and everything would be okay. I closed my eyes and prayed, and when I opened them again, my heart almost stopped as I saw his door open. I bit my bottom lip, excitement building inside of me, and I was just about to run to the door to meet him when he paused with one foot on my driveway. He stood there for a few minutes, looking at the house, then hung his head and climbed back into his truck, shut his door, and reversed out of the driveway. My heart sank as I watched him drive away.

I pulled my cell phone out of my pocket and pulled up his contact information. All I had to do was press the call button and tell him to come back. I'd even beg if I had to. My stomach flipped every time my finger hovered over that button, knowing he was that close, but so far away. Then the memory of him shutting his truck door and reversing out of the driveway hit, and I threw my phone down onto the chair I stood beside.

It was over, whatever it was. I just needed to accept it and move on. What we had, was it. I walked out into the hall and looked around, then shut the light off and climbed the stairs to my bedroom. I slipped out of my clothes and climbed into my cold bed. I curled up with the extra pillows and buried my face into the cold sheets.

Maddox

One Week Later

We'd been back for nearly a week, and I had not heard a word from Tess. I couldn't even begin to describe how much I missed her. I climbed into my truck after work and pulled my cell phone from my jacket pocket and checked for any messages, but there were none. I'd hoped that she would come around, and as I pulled up the last message she had sent me, it had been at the airport the morning we'd left for Paris when she had gotten lost in the airport trying to find the bathroom. I smiled at the memory and pocketed my phone, then fired up the engine and drove out of the lot.

    I drove through the snow-covered streets of town,

finally coming to the breakfast diner I'd agreed to meet a couple friends at for breakfast. I found a parking spot and cut the engine, once again checking my phone. I'd swore I felt it vibrate in my pocket, but there was nothing.

Irritation grew in me, then I realized I really had no right to be irritated; I hadn't tried to contact her. She certainly wasn't a mind reader, I thought. Perhaps this was just her way of letting me know we needed to go our separate ways. Yet an aching deep down in my stomach refused to believe that was true. Everything about me wanted more of her. I'd always found her attractive, but when I met her, she was already with Derrick, and unlike him, I had a fucking conscious.

I blew out a breath and ran my hand through my hair, then leaned back against my seat. Perhaps she just needed some time to figure out things, I thought to myself.

I checked my phone one more time, then pocketed it, pulling my keys from the ignition. If I didn't hear from her by Friday, I'd call her, I agreed with myself. I climbed out of my truck and made my way into the diner.

I spotted Tom and Pace sitting in the booth against the far wall and made my way over to them. "There he is," Tom said, smiling.

"Hey," I said sliding into the booth beside Pace.

"So? How the hell was the trip?" Tom asked.

Both Tom and Pace were the only two people who knew I had gone to Paris with Tess. Even though they, too, were friends with Derrick, I knew they could keep it to themselves.

"It was amazing," I answered as the server poured me a coffee.

"Do any sightseeing?"

"We did. You didn't mention anything to anyone, did you?" I asked, suddenly feeling a little on edge.

"You know us better than that. You asked us not to say anything," Tom answered.

"Besides, he was down south with that little number he's gotten involved with. Last we heard, they had a miserable time together." Pace chuckled. "I guess she dumped his ass on New Year's Eve. Looks good on him, actually." Pace picked up his mug and took a drink of his coffee while reading over the menu.

"Serves him right. You don't think he's going to be sniffing back around Tess, do you?" I asked, feeling concerned.

"Wouldn't surprise me. The man is incapable of not having a piece of ass," Tom answered, looking over my shoulder, a frown lining his face.

"So, how was the skiing?" Pace asked.

"Amazing. I highly recommend you guys take the wives and go sometime. Seriously, I think they were the best hills I've ever been on, and the view from the room was amazing. We actually had our own private chalet."

"Where do we need to go?" I heard a familiar voice ask from behind me.

I didn't even need to turn around to know who was standing behind me. I knew who that voice belonged to, and I hoped he hadn't heard what I said as a surge of anger flowed through me. I looked to both Pace and Tom before Derrick appeared in front of me and slid into the booth across from me. *What was Derrick doing here?* It was supposed to just be Tom, Pace, and me, but as I looked to my friends, I noticed they were just as surprised as I was to see him there.

"So, what did I miss? Where the fuck you go?" Derrick questioned, looking me straight in the eyes as if he actually knew where I had gone and was waiting to hear me say it.

A funny feeling ran over me at the fact that I sat across from someone who I once considered my best friend. Then Tess flashed through my mind, followed by the thought that only a week ago, I had been between Tess's legs. I shrugged. "I was just telling them about the ski trip I went on over to Breckenridge," I lied.

"Oh fuck, hell, I've skied there before. Not really anything special enough to write home about," Derrick replied, taking a sip of his freshly poured coffee.

"Maybe not to you, but I thought it was outstanding," I shot back, my insides stirring at his arrogance.

"What else did you do while you were there? Any cute snow bunnies?" Derrick questioned. "Oh wait, I forgot, you don't do that." He rolled his eyes and then laughed, elbowing Tom in the side.

Tom cleared his throat as Derrick continued to laugh at what he thought was a funny joke. "Anyways, everyone have a good holiday?" he asked, trying to steer the topic.

"Not too bad," Pace answered. "Busy with family as always. What about you Derrick?"

"Doesn't the tan say it all? Lucy and I spent two weeks down south."

"And how was that?" Tom asked, knowing full well that none of us really wanted to hear his answer.

"Let's put it this way... I wished I had been single."

"Shocking," I said under my breath as I clenched my jaw at his answer and picked up my mug, my knuckles turning white. He was already up to his old tricks.

"What did you say?" he asked, looking over at me.

I shook my head and took another sip of my coffee. "Nothing."

"Seriously, you guys should have seen the honeys. Fuck me. It was pussy everywhere."

I glared at Derrick as he sat there smiling away as he whined to the three of us about not being able to touch another woman because Lucy had kept him on a short leash. "I swear I couldn't even go to the bathroom without her."

"Do you blame her?" I bit out.

"What the fuck is that supposed to mean?" Derrick

asked, looking me right in the eyes, anger radiating off him.

Tom and Pace sat there, both uncomfortable as Derrick and I glared at one another. I wanted to shout out at him but knew it wouldn't be good if we caused a scene.

"How did you spend the new year?" Tom asked Pace, trying hard to disperse the tension that had now found its way to the table.

Pace went first, telling us about the party he and his wife had gone to. When it came to Derrick, he placed his mug down on the table and wiped his face. "It was pretty awful. First, Lucy and I had a huge fight. She stormed off to the room while I stayed out in the lobby. It was rocky the entire way home with her. She accused me of being unfaithful that night because I never went back to the room, and she has asked that I don't come around for a while. If that wasn't bad enough, I found out that Tess took the trip to Paris with some fucking guy, and when I messaged her, she refused to tell me who she was there with. All she did was keep telling me it was none of my concern."

The entire table went silent, and I lifted my head out of my phone and looked straight at Derrick. My mind flashed back to her standing outside on the patio New Year's Eve, feverishly typing away on her phone to someone. Derrick had been the someone, I'd been right, and anger flowed through me as I thought of the look on her face when I'd asked her if everything had been okay.

"Yep, you heard me. She cried and cried about a broken heart, and then I find out she was gallivanting across Europe with some fucking asshole, all smiles and shit."

"How do you know that?" Tom asked, looking to me.

"I had booked a dinner for us the night we were supposed to arrive. I'd given my credit card to hold the reservation, and when I checked my card, I saw the charge on my card. They charged a three-hundred-and-fifty-dollar meal to my card."

I laughed inside while trying to keep a straight face. Served him right.

"You think that's funny, do you?" Derrick asked, looking over at me. "I tell you when I find out who it was, I am going to tear him apart."

Both Tom and Pace looked to me and I to them. Double standards didn't work well in my books, and I was tired of listening to him. "Derrick, do you need to be reminded that you were the one who walked away from her. What difference does it make to you if she went to Paris with some guy? What did you expect her to do over the holidays, just sit around and mope, waiting for another chance with you, in case Lucy didn't work out?"

He shrugged. "Something like that." He chuckled, the arrogance pouring off him as he sat across from me. "So, if any of you hear who she went with, let me know. I'm going to pay him a visit."

"You are one arrogant fuck!" I gritted while both Tom and Pace sat there, their eyes wide.

"What the fuck is your problem, man?"

"You're my fucking problem." My eyes locked with Derrick as I stood up. I no longer saw a best friend; I saw an enemy. I clenched my fists and held my jaw tight. "You've always thought you could have the best of both worlds, always thought the grass was greener on the other side. Well, wake the fuck up, asshole. You gave her up for a piece of pussy, and by the looks of things, that is exactly what you got. I told you that the night I found you the first time with that slut from your office. I told you not to ruin something amazing, and you begged and pleaded with me not to tell Tess, because you said you knew I was right. So, I did what any best friend would do, and I protected your ass. I took your word, and you still fucked around on her. Now that things aren't going as amazing as they were with your new flavour of the week and you find out that Tess was, apparently, with someone else, you think you have the right to have a say in the matter. Well, wake the hell up because you don't."

"Fuck yourself," Derrick gritted, standing and shoving me in the chest.

I took two steps closer to him, getting up into his face,

and looked him square in the eyes. "Is that right? I should go fuck myself?"

"Yeah, you should, and you should also stay the fuck out of my personal life and keep your personal opinions to yourself. I've already told you that, but you keep sticking your nose where it doesn't belong," he said, poking me hard in my chest.

I chuckled under my breath and dropped my eyes to the floor as I thought of how to drop the bomb. I could see Derrick look around the diner, embarrassment written on his face as he noticed people staring at us. He held a high finance position in this town, and this was surely going to reflect badly on his reputation. He looked around at the people who sat in the diner, then held his hands up, smiling. "No need to worry, everyone. We are sorry. Just two old buddies going at it. It's all fine."

I looked up to see that he was no longer paying attention to me but looking and smiling at the few patrons of the diner who sat whispering to one another as they watched us. I brought my finger up and tapped him on the shoulder and waited until he turned to face me. Then I leaned into his ear and dropped the bomb.

"I have no problem staying out of your life. It's never been clearer to me exactly what kind of man you are, but I think you should know, if you want to have a round at the guy who went with Tess, let me know. I'll gladly tell you who it was."

Derrick blinked hard. "You know?" He took a moment to let the fact sink in that I knew who it was and hadn't told him. Then he cleared his throat. "Who was it?"

I looked at him a smirk coming to my face. "You're fucking looking at him," I growled, opening my arms wide.

"You?" he stammered. "How dare you!"

"How dare I what?" I yelled, getting up into his face.

Everyone in the diner froze as we stood eye-to-eye, neither of us backing down from one another. That was when my memory flashed back to us standing in the high school cafeteria in this exact position. We'd beaten the shit out of each other over a girl, only to both be turned down by the same girl a month later, and at that point, we had vowed never again to fight over another woman. Yet, somehow, almost fifteen years later, we stood in the same position. Only this time, it was different. The girl we were fighting over, I was in love with, and I was fully prepared to take the punch I was waiting for him to deliver. However, the punch never came. Instead, he turned and ripped his coat off the hook on the side of the booth and stormed out of the diner.

Tess

I studied the menu in front of me, trying to decide between either the southwest chicken salad or a green salad with salmon, while Laura finished her phone call with a new client. I'd just closed the menu and taken a sip of my wine when she tucked her phone into her purse. "So sorry about that. I knew I shouldn't have answered the call. Did you decide on something?"

"Think I'm going with the chicken," I said, putting my wine down and opening the menu again. "Or perhaps the pasta."

Laura laughed at my indecisiveness and quickly decided, closing her menu. "Okay now, I want to hear all about this trip. I've been bloody well dying."

I giggled. "Well, who on earth goes on a business trip

two days after the new year for a week? You should have been home."

"Hey, in my defence, it was supposed to be John who went. He had a family emergency, so I had to be a good co-worker and step up. Plus, it's one of the biggest accounts I've worked on, so the opportunity that it presented was way too good to pass up."

"So, things are going well then at this firm. That makes me happy. You deserve it. You've worked so hard." I smiled, taking another sip of wine.

"Yeah, yeah, sure. All right, so spill it. How was Paris?"

"It was absolutely breathtaking," I said, smiling. "Best decision I ever made was to take that trip, regardless of what happened between Derrick and me. I am so glad that you talked me into it."

"Aren't that what friends are for? To talk you into doing the things you don't really want to do but know you should do them?" Laura laughed.

"Can you not take a compliment?" I laughed. "That's it, I will not say anything else."

"Well, you are! Now, what about the food? Was it amazing?"

"Unbelievable. My God, the deserts were out of this world. Seriously, I am surprised I didn't gain a hundred pounds while I was gone," I said, picking up a slice of bread from the basket and ripping a piece off. "I honestly think it was the best part of every meal."

"I've heard desserts in Paris are amazing. Now what was your favourite?"

My mind flashed to Maddox sitting across from me, his eyes closed as he took the first bite of the crème brûlée. "I'd have to say the crème brûlée."

"And did you end up treating yourself and eat in the Eiffel Tower or did you just pass? I know you were so excited about that, and I swear if you tell me no after the way Derrick treated you over that, I think I may disown you. I swear if I had been in your shoes, I would have charged that dinner on the asshole's credit card. Make him pay for it, because I am sure it wasn't a cheap meal. Would have served him right."

A funny feeling came over me as I thought back to that night. That was the first night that Maddox had kissed me. I could still feel his lips on mine, still smell the scent of the cologne he wore as he leaned into me. I softly smiled. "Yes, it was beyond anything I ever could have imagined. The view, the food, everything was so perfect."

That description couldn't have been further from the truth. Everything had been perfect. When I finally pulled myself out of the memory, I looked over to my best friend who sat staring at me, a curious look on her face. She put her elbow on the table and then rested her chin on her hand.

"What?" I questioned.

"You look...hmmm...you look happy," she said,

squinting her eyes at me.

"So, I am happy. I just spent ten days in an absolutely beautiful city."

"Yes, you did, but you also just got your heart broken." She faltered, pointing at me with her fork.

I blinked at her words as if I had just realized it myself. Derrick had barely entered my mind since we'd returned. My head and heart had been consumed by Maddox. It was almost as if Derrick had never even existed.

"I guess I just figured that you would still be hurting."

I thought before I answered her, thinking back to Maddox and the night he had told me about his fiancée. A soft smile fell on my lips as his words flashed through my mind. I smiled. "I guess time has a way of healing a broken heart, and how fast it heals depends on how deep the wound was to begin with. I guess the wound wasn't as deep as I first thought." I shrugged.

Laura looked at me with a shocked expression. "What... the hell... happened to you?"

I shrugged. "Guess you could say I did a little soul searching while I was gone, and through that I learned a little about myself."

"Hmm, I see. A certain someone wouldn't have anything to do about that, would he?"

I swallowed hard and picked up my wine, just as our food arrived at the table and a bowl of pasta was slipped in front of me.

"Looks delicious," I said, picking up my fork and digging into my pasta.

"Oh no, no way. You're not getting away from that question," Laura said, looking over at me, a sly smile on her face. "Spill it."

The memory of Maddox holding me in his arms the last few nights of our trip flashed through my mind. My body instantly heated at the memory of his touch. I thought about the first time we had sex, how gentle and attentive he had been, how he made sure that every single time we had done it, I was comfortable with every step. He never once took anything for granted, nor did he make me feel as if I were just something he was trying to conquer. I felt all the emotion he carried in every touch, every glance, and every kiss he had bestowed upon me. I saw the way he looked at me afterward as well. There was never a moment that I doubted or regretted anything that had happened between us, just that I did not run down the walkway the night he dropped me at home. A warm feeling came over me as Laura sat and watched me, and I felt my cheeks heat as the realization hit me.

I blew out a breath as I nodded. "He might have." I smiled.

"Oh my God," Laura said, her jaw dropping.

"What?" I questioned, taking in her expression.

"Did you two...you know?"

I bit my bottom lip and nodded, completely unsure if

I should say anything at all, as a flood of excitement ran through my body.

"...and..."

That was when the realization hit me I knew how he felt about me. I wasn't sure what to call it, but I knew that I had pushed away possibly the greatest thing to ever happen to me because I was afraid. I was afraid of how intensely I felt about him. Never in my life had I had someone I ever felt that strongly about, not even Derrick, and I guess that was why I hadn't even thought of him since. I had spent all that time on the plane crying in his arms because I didn't want to let him go, only to realize that I didn't know how to tell him. He stood in the entryway of my house after he dropped me off, tension and silence building between us because he didn't know how to tell me either.

"... and I threw it all away because I didn't know how to tell him how I felt," I said as a heavy weight descended on my chest.

Laura looked down at the table, a smile coming to her lips. "I don't think you've thrown anything away. I think you just need to take a moment and organize your thoughts and then call that deliciously sexy man and tell him you want him."

I shook my head. "No, Laura, it's way too late," I said, pulling my fork through my pasta.

"You only think that, but, Tess, if you don't tell him,

in five years, you'll be regretting that choice. So, I think you should do it today, right after lunch. Perhaps in the car on the way back home." She winked.

I couldn't help but giggle as excitement filled me. "He makes me happy."

"I can tell." Laura laughed, picking up her fork and digging into her salad. "Do you think he feels the same way?"

"I do. I really do," I murmured.

"All right then, so if you know he feels that way, then what are you so afraid of. We are going to treat this lunch as a work meeting because we need to hatch a plan. I want you ready when you leave here, I want you to feel confident and go out there and get that man."

Laura and I had finished our Friday afternoon lunch at two, and before she would let me leave the restaurant, she had scribbled something on a sheet of paper, folded it up, and shoved it at me. "Here, this is your plan. Put it in your purse. Don't look at it, and if you get home and sit down to call him and get nervous, only then can you read what I wrote." She giggled, shoving the folded piece of paper into my hand.

I'd driven home feeling amazing and full of confidence, but as the day had passed, those feelings faded, and all of my insecurities came flooding back full force.

It was a little after four, and I sat curled up in my chair in the living room, a hot cup of tea sitting beside me. I glanced across the living room and saw something sitting underneath a pile of bills on my corner desk. I went over shoved the bills aside and smiled as I looked down at the picture of Maddox and me from the airport that he had framed. I couldn't help but smile as I looked at him. The happiness in his eyes as he hugged me close, waiting for me to snap the picture. I set the frame on the table beside my mug of hot tea, and then I reached for the phone. I was so nervous my hand shook. *Just breathe,* I whispered to myself as I began to dial his number.

I was just about to dial the last number when someone knocked on the door. I frowned. I wasn't expecting anybody, I thought, making my way to the front door. I pulled the door open, and all the blood drained from my face. Derrick stood there, his coat wrapped tightly around him.

"Tess, can I come in?" he asked, shivering.

I was too shocked to say anything. Instead I just stepped to the side and let him in. I closed the door behind him and took a step back, crossing my arms over my chest.

"It's good to see you," he said, smiling.

"What do you want, Derrick?" I asked, looking at the

lying, cheating, pathetic man who stood in front of me.

"I've come to talk."

"About what? What could we possibly have to talk about?" I asked, growing annoyed, thinking back to his messages on New Year's Eve. How mean, cruel, and demanding he had been with me.

"Us."

I let out a laugh. "Us? You've got to be kidding me. If you want to talk about an us, why don't you go talk to your little side piece. Oh wait, let me guess, you can't because she kicked you to the curb. She grew tired of your games, and you are here to see if you can get me back," I said as bitterness filled my mouth.

"I made a mistake. I didn't realize how good I had it with you," he pleaded.

I rolled my eyes as I stood staring at the man that I'd once thought I'd loved. Now looking at him, even I did not know what it was I'd seen in him. "Little bit to late for that, don't you think?"

"Tess, please, just give me a chance to explain."

I held my hand out in front of me to stop him. "Derrick, I'm sorry, but I don't have that kind of time. You threw me to the curb, remember, and if I remember your words correctly, you were in love with someone else. No, that wasn't it. You found someone who was perfect," I said, searching my memory for his words. "Anyways, it was something like that, wasn't it? Well, you got your wish, now you got her," I said, crossing my arms across my chest, glancing between him and the door, hoping he would take the hint and leave.

"Tess, please," he begged

Rage filled me the more he stood there begging. "You know, Derrick, I, too, made a mistake. My mistake was never cutting you loose the first time you cheated on me."

Derrick looked at me, a realization coming to his face that I had known about him and his secretary.

"That's right, I knew, and if you thought for one second I didn't know about that, you are wrong. I knew, and I never said a word to you. Call it denial, call it stupidity, or perhaps we will say I was hoping that you might realize what you were doing and make a change, but obviously you didn't. Instead, you just became better at hiding it, at lying to me. So you see, you aren't the only one who made a mistake. The problem is, I could take you back right now, but you will always be the same, no matter what you say or how much you promise you're going to change. You could be faithful for six months to a year, but eventually the urge to cheat on me will come around again." I crossed my arms and stood there, waiting for him to turn around.

The phone began to ring, and I glanced to the living room, my heart beating hard as I wondered if that call was Maddox.

"I guess that is my cue," he said in a low voice.

"Yes, besides, I've got to get that," I said, stepping toward him to try and push him out the door, but he didn't move.

"Wait, is it true, Tess?" he asked, hanging his head.

"Is what true?"

"Did you go to Paris…with…Maddox?" he questioned, lifting his head and meeting my eyes.

I looked at Derrick. I was sure it was hurt I saw in his eyes. I blew out a breath and ran my fingers through my hair, unsure if I should tell him the truth or not, but decided that by not telling him would make me just as bad as he was. I looked into his eyes; he did deserve to know the truth. "Yes." I nodded. "We went to Paris."

He stood there stiff with rage. "You went on our honeymoon with my best friend?" His voice cracked.

I nodded as anxiety snaked through my body. "It wasn't our honeymoon after you left, Derrick." My insides shook as we stood in the hallway, our eyes locked as he digested the information.

"He'll never be right for you, Tess. He can't offer you the same security I can."

I stood there, my mind going a million miles a minute. I shook my head. "You're wrong about that." I swallowed hard, fighting back tears. "Maddox, is ten times the man you could ever wish to be. As for security, it's enough to say that knowing he isn't out dicking around with every chick who walks by him is all the security I need."

"Did you sleep with him?" he demanded.

I felt a rage build in me at his question. He had no right to ask me that because I knew exactly where he was going with this. He was going to claim that I, too, had cheated and that I was no better than he was, but I wasn't going to stand for it. "Derrick, it's time you leave, now," I said, pointing to the door.

"You did, didn't you?" he pressed, trying to get me to answer. "You fucked him on that trip? Or perhaps the two of you were fucking far before that, huh?"

My eyes locked on his, and before I could stop myself, I reached out and slapped him across the face. Instantly, he brought his hand up to cover his cheek.

"Are you going to answer me? Did you fuck my best friend?"

"Get out!" I gritted, rage filling my body.

"Do you have feelings for him?" he pushed.

"Like I said, he is ten times the man you could ever hope to be," I whispered and looked away, avoiding eye contact. I didn't need to answer him because he already knew.

He stood there for a few moments, watching me, then he cleared his throat. "Good-bye, Tess." He turned, pulled the door open ,and stepped out into the cold, shutting the door behind him.

I stood there for a moment, trying to dispel the tension in my body as silence fell around me.

Maddox

I'd promised myself that if I had not heard from her by Friday, I would make the move. I sat in my truck outside of the fire station, freshly showered, and hung up my cell phone. There was no answer. I glanced over to my passenger's seat and looked down at the fresh bouquet that sat wrapped on my seat. I debated calling again, but then decided to drive over there to see her instead.

I shoved my key into the ignition and turned the engine over and reversed out of the spot. It took me twenty minutes to drive across the city, and a smile spread over my face as I saw her car in its usual spot in the driveway. I cut my lights before I pulled in beside her car. I didn't want to notify her I was here. I wanted it to be a surprise. I grabbed the bouquet from the passenger's seat and made my way to the front door and rang the bell.

"Go away, Derrick," I heard Tess call from inside the house.

I frowned. What the hell had Derrick been doing here? I wondered and rang the bell again.

"Why can't you take a hint," her words echoed from inside.

This time, instead of ringing the bell, I raised my hand and knocked hard on the door.

"Derrick, I told you to go… away." Her words stopped the second her eyes landed on me. "Maddox? What are you…" she asked, looking down at the wrapped bouquet I held in my hands and back to my eyes, then she stepped back and opened the door.

"Everything okay?" I asked as I stepped inside, my eyes washing over her, the sudden want to protect her filling me.

"Yes, everything is fine." She smiled and nodded. I held the flowers out to her. She reached out and took the flowers, her fingers grazing mine, and a wave of desire flickered to life inside me. She removed the wrapper and buried her nose into the bouquet of carnations. "These are beautiful, thank you." She smiled.

"You're welcome. So, what was going on?"

"Nothing, Derrick showed up."

"Ah. Everything okay?" I asked while watching her twirl a strand of hair around her forefinger.

"You wouldn't believe me if I told you anyways," she

said, waving her hand dismissing the subject. "Anyway, what are you doing here? I wasn't expecting to see you so soon," she admitted as I followed her into the kitchen.

I watched as she grabbed a vase from under the counter and filled it, then placed the flowers into it and set it in the middle of the table.

"Well, I thought I would come by and see if you wanted to go for dinner?" I asked, letting out a deep breath, trying to fight being nervous as I waited for her answer. "There is a new French place over on Fifth that I thought we could try," I said, approaching her, unsure if I should touch her.

She looked up at me, a soft smile coming to her lips. "That sounds wonderful," she whispered.

I nodded. "Hmm, yes, it does," I whispered as our eyes locked. "You, what else sounds wonderful?"

She bit her bottom lip as she stepped into me and placed her hands on my chest, looking up into my eyes, waiting for me to speak.

"The sound of your yes when I ask you to come back to my place tonight," I replied, pushing a strand of hair from her eyes. I didn't wait for her to answer. Instead I just lowered my mouth to hers and took her in my arms.

"Anyway, so he showed up at my door tonight and practically begged me to allow him to explain his wrongdoings." She laughed as she took a sip of her wine.

"I can't get over that. However, I know you gave him the time to do that, didn't you?" I said, looking at her with a mischievous glint in my eye, knowing full well she wanted nothing more to do with him.

"Yep, of course. I gave him just long enough to give him a piece of my mind and kick him out. Of course, he never could take a hint very well, and after he stood staring at me, giving me those big puppy eyes, he finally left. Then you arrived. I figured it was him begging me again." She giggled and then grew quiet. "How have you been?"

"I've been good. Working mostly. What about you?"

"Same," she said, meeting my eyes.

As she sat across from me, I couldn't get over how beautiful she was. She had been the only thing on my mind since the night I pulled from her driveway, and I'd been a damn fool for not getting out of the damn truck and going back in that house that night. Now that she sat in front of me, I was almost afraid to breathe in case one wrong breath made her disappear. I reached across the table and took hold of her hand in mine, my thumb running across the back of her hand as I looked into her eyes.

"I've missed you...," we both said in unison, both of us lowering our eyes at our admission.

I watched as a small smile came to her lips as she rose her eyes to mine. "I should have called!" she exclaimed.

"No, I should have called," I insisted and we both laughed.

Her tongue jutted out and licked her lips. She was about to say something when "Easy on Me" by Adele began playing. This song brought me back to New Year's Eve as I held her in my arms and we danced together right before midnight. I grabbed her hand and stood up. "Come with me," I said, gently pulling her out of her seat.

"Maddox? What are you doing?"

"I want you to dance with me, come on," I urged.

"But, Maddox, no one else is dancing..." she said under her breath, looking around the restaurant.

"I don't care," I replied, pulling her into my arms. "So now, tell me, why didn't you call?" I asked as we swayed back and fourth.

"It's silly."

"Tell me."

"I was scared. I wasn't sure that you felt the same."

I couldn't help but chuckle at her answer. I was so in love with this woman, it wasn't funny.

"What's so funny about that? Why didn't you call me then?" she asked with fire in her voice.

"I only laugh because I didn't call for the same reason," I said, pulling her into me, holding her close.

"Oh." A soft smile landed on her lips, and then she

rested her head against my chest as we swayed to the music.

"I figured that because you'd just ended things with Derrick, that perhaps you needed more time to digest everything. I wasn't sure if what happened between us on that trip was because you were trying to bury the pain of what happened, or because you were truly interested. There were a few times it seemed that words just hung between us, and to be honest, I was afraid that if I began to tell you the way I felt it would scare you off. Plus, I certainly didn't want you to think I was trying to take advantage of the situation because you were in a vulnerable state."

She raised her eyes to mine and studied me for a moment. Then she raised up on her toes and placed a kiss on my lips. "You would be the last person that I would think would take advantage of me. You aren't like his other friends. To be honest, I was petrified at first of what was going on between us, but I'm not scared anymore. I spent a lot of time searching myself, and knowing how I felt the day we boarded the plane to come home and this past week has given me the time to know that am ready. I don't want to waste any more time rehashing the past. He isn't worth my time, he never was, and had I realized that the first time he'd cheated on me with his secretary, things would be so much different."

"Wait, you knew about the secretary?" He frowned, looking down into my eyes.

"Of course, I did, and before you drive yourself crazy, I am not angry with you for not telling me. I knew when I sent you there that night. The only person I am angry at now is myself for not saying anything to him when he came home smelling of her perfume, and for not questioning him when I found the smear of lipstick on his collar. Instead, I turned on my blinders and looked the other way. However, in order to allow myself to heal, I have to be forgiving of myself or else I will never ever love anyone again."

I pulled her in tighter and closed my eyes as she rested her head on my chest.

"I want to love you. You're the first thing I think of when I open my eyes in the morning, and I can't begin to tell you how empty I have felt without you around." She looked up at me with her eyes full of tears. "I want to be yours, all yours," she murmured.

"Then be mine," I whispered as I placed my hand on the back of her neck and pulled her in for a deep kiss.

"Maddox?" she whispered as our kiss broke, both of us breathless.

"Yeah?"

"Take me back to your place. Make me yours," she breathed, kissing my lips.

Tess

I sat in the front seat of his truck as he drove across town to his place. The instant the answer had fallen from my lips, he had requested the bill and paid. Seconds later, we were rushing out the door and across the parking lot toward his truck, and now it felt like we never going to get there as my body hummed with anticipation.

I sat watching as we passed by houses, my center throbbing with excitement. He finally pulled into his driveway and cut the engine. He looked over at me, hunger in his eyes, then he opened his door and walked to my side, helping me out, and then, hand-in-hand, we walked up the walkway. He struggled with his key, only for a second, finally pushing the door open.

"I'll give you the grand tour," he said as he shut the door behind us.

I'd barely gotten my shoes off when he grabbed me, pushing me up against the wall, attacking my mouth with his, his tongue forcing my lips apart and washing through my mouth with an urgent force. My entire body was on fire as I felt his arousal through his pants as he pressed his body into me.

"I've missed you," he whispered between kisses, his hands running through my hair.

I closed my eyes, kissing him back. "I missed you too."

He wrapped his arms around me, pulling me tighter into him. His hands ran down my body, cupping my ass. He grabbed the bottom of my shirt and I lifted my arms above my head so he could pull it over my head, dropping it to a pile on the floor. I did the same, pulling his shirt over his head, dropping it into the same heap as mine and pushed myself against his hot skin.

He kissed my mouth with urgency, moving to my neck before kissing the top of my breasts. He ran his thumbs over breasts, my nipples hardening at his touch. He bit both nipples through my bra, while I reached down, running my hand over the large bulge in the front of his jeans. He let out a deep, throaty growl as I pulled at his belt and then gripped his cock again through his jeans. "Fuck, Tess, we've got to slow down."

"I don't want to slow down. I want you to take me, please. Just take me...hard and rough," I pleaded, sucking his earlobe into my mouth.

"Fuck it," he muttered, placing his hands under my ass and picking me up, carrying me down the hall as he attacked my mouth. Dropping me on the bed, he unbuttoned my pants, then he roughly pulled both my jeans and panties off me. He unbuttoned his pants, letting them fall to the floor, and then dropped to his knees as he spread my legs and attacked my center.

I laced my fingers through his hair as he licked and sucked me into his mouth, my climax building fast.

"You're sexy as hell," he said, attacking my center again.

I closed my eyes and arched my back as he continued his assault, then felt pressure at my opening and cried out as he slid two thick fingers inside of me. He continued licking and gently sucking as he pumped his fingers deeply into me.

"Maddox... please...stop..." I cried, afraid I could no longer hold back.

Instead of listening, he continued, and when I tightened around his fingers, he quickly pulled out, opened my legs wider, and placed himself at my opening, shoving his way into me. I cried out and gripped his arms as he started pumping into me hard and deep.

He buried himself as far as he could, bending down to kiss me. He moved his lips over me and then surprised me by pulling himself out. I went to beg him to come back but didn't have a chance to get the words out because he shoved himself back inside of me rough and deep, the sound of our skin slapping. I cried out as he did it again and again. He took my mouth with his and allowed me to come back down, only to pull out and quickly shove himself back into me.

I cried out and clenched around him tightly, gripping his biceps as he continued to repeat his movements. He slowed down as I clung to him and pulled himself from me.

He gripped my hips and rolled me over, pulling me back to the edge of the bed. He ran his hands over my ass, giving me a playful tap, before he kissed my shoulder. He gripped my shoulder and lined himself at my entrance and slid into me hard and deep, holding me in place. He was rough and raw, and he took me, every last part of me, right there in his bedroom. We climaxed together, and then we collapsed onto the bed, both of us breathless.

He held me in his arms afterward and brushed my hair back out of my face and looked into my eyes as he kissed me, slow and deep.

"I love you," he whispered as he kissed my neck.

I bit my bottom lip, every part of me tensing at his words, my stomach flopping at his admission. I, too, felt the same way, and when he raised himself up and looked down into my eyes, I knew I had to tell him, "I love—"

I didn't even get the words out as he attacked my mouth. I could feel him growing hard again, only this time he slid on top of me as I parted my legs to accommodate him. I felt him reach down between us, lining himself at my opening, and slid himself inside slow and deep. This time there was no roughness, nothing raw. This was different from all the other times. This time he made love to me, and as the sweat poured off him, our moans filled the room and we climaxed together.

Maddox

October 15

"The house just went up for sale!" She exclaimed.

"That's awesome, baby." I smiled to myself. I was so ready to continue on this amazing journey that we had begun that I could barely hide my excitement.

"Yep, the agent just left. She assured me it should sell rather quickly."

I could hear the happiness in her voice, and it filled me with a warmth I hadn't felt in a long time.

"So, I guess that means you'd better start packing."

"Oh, yeah, I sort of forgot about that." She giggled. "Did you want to come by after work and give me a hand?"

I smiled to myself at the excitement in her voice. Things had been going so well between us, and when we found we were spending all of our time with one another, it no longer made sense for us both to keep our own places. She agreed, and since my place was bigger, she agreed to put hers on the market.

"I can, but you better get a head start because, if I know us, we probably won't get a ton of packing done once I get there." We'd never been able to keep our hands off one another. we were like teenagers whenever we got together.

Her laughter filled my ear. "You are so bad." She giggled.

"Okay, sweetie, I've got to run. I'll be right over after work. Love you."

"Love you too. be safe."

I hung up from the call, pocketing my phone, and pulled my truck into a parking spot in front of the store I'd been heading to. I cut the engine and leaned forward, looking up at the dark-blue sign, and swallowed hard. *Maddison Jewelers.* I never thought that this day would come again for me. I took a minute, debating on calling Tom or Pace to see if they could meet me here, but then changed my mind. I hadn't mentioned anything to anyone that I was doing this. I figured it was better this way. I took a breath and climbed out of the truck, a knot forming in my stomach, and made my way to the door.

The little bells that hung on the top of the door jingled away as I pulled the door open, notifying the clerks that they had a new customer. A girl looked up from the counter and smiled at me. She was busy with another customer and asked them to give her a minute. "Can I help you with something?" She asked.

I stepped inside and walked over to the counter. "I'm wondering if you could show me some engagement rings?" I asked, swallowing hard. The couple she was serving looked up at me and I gave them both a nervous smile.

"Sure, they are right over in that display across the way. Give me a few minutes and I will be right over."

I nodded and made my way over to the case she'd directed me to. I looked down at all the unique rings. There were so many options, and I was a lot lost as to what she would even like. I knew what her previous engagement ring looked like, and I wanted to steer clear of that as I'd come to learn that she hated the thing.

"They are beautiful, aren't they?" the salesclerk said, coming over and opening the back of the display case.

I nodded, finally seeing one that I knew in my heart was perfect. "Could I see that one in the corner please?"

"The solitaire?" she questioned, reaching into the case, pointing at the ring.

"Yes, please."

"Wonderful choice. It's my favourite. Although I can't

seem to get my boyfriend to commit." She giggled as she placed the ring in my hand. "White gold band, diamond is colourless and flawless. I believe it's the best one we have in the store at the moment."

The girl droned on, and I eventually shut her out while I looked down at the ring. It was beautiful and simple, yet elegant, exactly like my girl. I looked up at the girl who was still speaking away and smiled. "I'll take it."

November 30 – 6 Weeks Later

White Christmas lights twinkled brightly in the trees around the manmade rink in the park. Tess sat on the bench while I knelt before her, holding the skate. She held onto the top of her sock as she pushed her foot inside.

"How's that?" I asked, making sure that her foot was all the way in.

"It's okay, but I don't know about this, Maddox," she said, a worried expression lining her face as I pulled at the laces, tightening them for her.

I looked up at her and smiled. "Do you trust me?" I questioned, repeating the same steps with the other skate.

"Of course." She laughed. "It's just the whole sliding and balance issue, remember."

"I remember." I chuckled and sat down beside her, quickly lacing up my own skates. "I'm going to have you skating circles around me before you know it."

"I seriously doubt that." She laughed, looking down at her skates.

I reached into my pocket and felt the velvet box I had tucked inside earlier. "Here, put your gloves on," I said, handing over her the gloves she'd placed inside the bag for tonight. She slid her hands inside and I stood, holding my hands out to her.

She slid her hands into mine and stood. I didn't give her any time to back out. I stepped onto the ice and held onto her as she placed one foot on the ice and then the other.

She wobbled for a minute as she held onto my shoulders, finally steadying herself.

"All right, so you can stand," I teased.

She gave me an annoyed look. "Of course I can stand." Then she laughed.

"All right, let's go. Just push off with one foot. Like this, watch," I said, pushing off with one foot and sliding a bit of a ways away from her.

"Oh, I don't know." She hesitated, her voice shaky as she looked at me.

"You can do it," I urged, watching as she tried to find

the courage within herself. She concentrated hard and shoved off with one foot, then the other. She was doing okay making her way toward me, when she suddenly lost her balance, her arms flailed about, her face filled with panic. I reached out and grabbed her, breaking her fall just before she went down.

"Oh my God," she yelled, as she reached out and grabbed hold of me.

I laughed while steadying us both, holding onto her tightly as she regained her balance.

"I told you I can't do this," she said, breathing hard, frustration lining her face.

"It's not happening overnight, baby. It takes time. You'll get it, I promise." I moved around her until I was behind her, and placed my hands on her hips. Then I slowly pushed off and began gliding around the rink with her in front of me.

We had the entire rink to ourselves, so once I had gotten her comfortable enough, I began the lesson all over again, and by the time we were ready to go, she could skate off the rink just holding onto my hand.

"Did you see that? I did it," she said, excitement lining her voice. She looked proud of herself, and once she was on the bench, I knelt down in the snow and pulled her skates off.

"I did. You were amazing, baby."

"I'd hardly call me amazing." She giggled, slipping her feet into her boots.

I sat down beside her and removed my skates. Then I reached down into our bag and pulled out a thermos along with two travel cups and poured us each a hot chocolate.

"Here you go," I said, handing her one of the travel mugs. I capped the thermos and leaned back against the bench, placing my arm behind her.

I watched as her eyes light up as she took a sip. "Maddox, this isn't..."

"It is, right from that place in the mall. They opened up another location around the corner from work, so I stopped on my way home to get this." I smiled, leaning in to kiss her lips.

Over the past year, I learned so many things about Tess I hadn't known before. How much she could give when she felt appreciated. How feisty she could be when she got angry, how sexy she could be when she let her inhibitions go. There wasn't a part of this woman I didn't love. I learned that she loved the simple things in life—a homemade meal and an evening with popcorn and a movie, instead of dinner in a fancy restaurant, a foot rub and hot bath after a long day, instead of being pampered at the spa. The best thought was waking her with a tender kiss and a hot coffee in the morning after we'd spent the night making love. However, my favourite part of this past year had been watching her discover herself as our relationship developed. Watching her become a woman filled with confidence and one who never backed down from me when I got out of line. It had been a special gift that she had given to me. The Tess I had met a few years ago was not the same woman who sat beside me today. She was confident and loving, and she was all mine.

"When's my next lesson?" he asked, leaning her head against my shoulder and cuddling into my side.

I placed a kiss on her forehead and smiled. "Whenever you'd like."

"Tomorrow?" She laughed, biting her bottom lip as she looked up at me.

"Mmmm, I think we might be busy tomorrow." I chuckled, reaching into my pocket.

She frowned. I could see her mentally searching through her schedule trying to figure out what I was talking about.

I sat forward and pulled the box out of my pocket and turned to face her.

"Maddox, I don't know what you are talking about," she said, still trying to figure out what plans she had forgotten. "The only thing we have this week is dinner with Laura and John. I am sure of it."

I let out a breath as she sat there mumbling our schedule repeatedly to herself. I chuckled to myself, trying to ease my own nerves, then placed my hand over hers.

"Tess, I just figured that you might want to go out and celebrate."

She looked at me, frowning. "Maddox, I don't know what you are talking about. Celebrate what? If you're talking about me learning to skate, you're just being silly." She laughed, placing her hand on my arm and giving me a gentle shove.

I flipped open the box and brought it around for her to see. "I thought we'd celebrate our engagement."

Her eyes went from mine down to the ring that sat in my hand, and then she brought her hand up to her mouth, tears filling her eyes. I smiled, tears filling my own. "Will you marry me, Tess?" I questioned, pulling the ring from the small box. She placed her hand in mine, and I slid the ring onto her finger.

She wrapped her arms around my neck and placed a kiss on my lips. "Yes," she murmured. "Oh my God, yes."

Tess

We lay in bed together, wrapped securely in blankets as the morning sun peered through the blinds. I lay in his arms, my hand resting on his chest so I could look down at the ring on my finger. I must have looked at it a million times since he'd given it to me last night. I was still having a hard time believing that it had actually happened. That he had finally asked me to marry him. I softly smiled at the thought.

"What are you thinking about?" he asked quietly, running his finger along my bare arm.

"Last night," I replied, as I enjoyed the warmth of his body as I lay beside him.

"What about it?" he asked, shifting himself so he was looking down on me.

I shrugged. "Just how perfect it was." I met his eyes

and as he looked longingly down on me, my eyes beginning to water.

"Yeah, it's a beautiful rink isn't it. The lights in the trees and all..." He looked at me seriously.

"Stop it." I laughed. "You know what I'm talking about."

He nodded and lowered himself and took my mouth with his, kissing me deeply, his tongue washing through my mouth. "It was perfect," he whispered, gripping my waist with his hand.

He pulled his lips from mine and brushed my hair back out of my face. I reached up and ran my fingers through his hair, studying him.

I loved this man with my entire soul, and no number of words would ever allow me to express that to him the way I wished I could. He had taught me so much about myself over the past year that it was hard to remember what I was like before. He had taught me all over again that it was okay to love, and to not be afraid to express my feelings. He'd also taught me what it felt like to be appreciated and valued. The amount of love we shared was above and beyond what I'd ever experienced.

He kissed me deeply, his hands running down my body as he pulled me close to him. We fit so perfectly together. I thought back to that trip to Paris. If it hadn't of been for that, who knows where I would be. Would I have been in his arms? Perhaps, but it may have taken us way longer to find one another. There hadn't been a day that had passed since we'd returned from Paris that I didn't silently thank myself for listening to Laura and my mom for actually making me take that trip. I also silently thanked Maddox for agreeing to go.

He pulled away from my lips, breathless, his rigid cock ready for more. "Now about that lesson?"

I couldn't help but laugh. "I think we should stay right here," I whispered, meeting his lips. "You can give me a different type of lesson," I suggested with a knowing look.

"I couldn't agree more. I'm one lucky man," he whispered.

Epilogue

TESS

Looking back, if someone had told me last Christmas that just by taking a simple trip at the lowest time in my life that everything would change, I wouldn't have believed them. When I boarded that plane, I never thought it was going to be possible for me to ever trust or love again. I felt absolutely dead inside. Yet something magical happened on that trip. A man I loved as a friend and confident taught me that, no matter how much hurt a person endures, it is possible for time to heal everything. He had overcome a substantial loss himself, and time had allowed him to heal; the same had been true for me.

I don't even think I need to tell you that Derrick had never been the one for me. He hadn't been the one for Lucy either, Francine, or Nicky. The last we'd heard; his business was failing so he'd packed up his life here and left the city.

I'd finally told Maddox about him coming to me the night before he showed up at my door and all he had said. He listened to every word I had said and then told me about the display in the diner. Tom and Pace both agreed that after that event, his reputation had gone right downhill. The women who used to give him the time of day no longer looked at him, and others no longer wanted to do business after they learned what had really happened between him and me. They said they didn't want to work with a womanizer.

Maddox and I spent our first Christmas together surrounded by friends and family. Three years later, we welcomed a new addition to our family. Noelle Rose was born December 19th during a wicked snowstorm. She was perfect and looked exactly like her father.

I stood just outside the nursery on Christmas Eve, the house quiet, watching as Maddox held this tiny little human in his arms, rocking her gently in the wee hours of the morning, even though he had worked all day just so I could get my sleep.

Our life, for now, was complete, and as I watched him and listened to her gentle coo as he spoke to her in a soft voice, a peacefulness came over me. Fate had blessed me, all because I allowed time to heal my broken heart and I learned to trust again. It was the greatest gift I'd ever given to myself.

A Note from the Author

Dear Readers,

I would like to thank you for taking the time to read *The Greatest Gift*. I would like to thank the members of my reader group Sterling's Silver Sapphires for helping me name the hero of this story. If you loved The Greatest Gift please take a moment and drop me a review. I always love to hear what my readers think.

Soundtrack for The Greatest Gift

Traitor - Olivia Rodrigo
Only You - Yazoo
Knowing You - Kenny Chesney
Easy on Me - Adele

Coming Soon from S.L. Sterling

Doctor Desire (Doctors of Eastport General) March 4, 2022
Ace (Book 2 Vegas MMA) Release Date Coming Soon
Blade (Book 3 Vegas MMA) Release Date Coming Soon

About the Author

S.L. Sterling had been an avid reader since she was a child, often found getting lost in books. Today if she isn't writing or plotting, she can be found buried in a romance novel. S.L. Sterling lives with her husband and dog in Northern Ontario.

Visit my Website to learn more, or sign up for my Newsletter to stay in touch.

Join my Reader Group
Sterlings Silver Sapphires

Other Titles by S.L. Sterling

Standalones

It Was Always You

On A Silent Night

Bad Company

Back to You this Christmas

Fireside Love

Holiday Wishes

All I Want for Christmas

All American Boys Series

Saviour Boy

The Boy Under the Gazebo

The Malone Brother Series

A Kiss Beneath the Stars

In Your Arms

His to Hold

Finding Forever with You

Vegas MMA

Dagger

KB Worlds: Everyday Heroes

Constraint

CPSIA information can be obtained
at www.ICGtesting.com
Printed in the USA
BVHW030446101221
623703BV00001B/16